TOR BOOKS BY AMAL EL-MOHTAR

The River Has Roots

SEASONS
OF GLASS
AND IRON

SEASONS OF GLASS AND IRON

Stories

AMAL EL-MOHTAR

TOR PUBLISHING GROUP
NEW YORK

This is a work of fiction. All of the names, characters, organizations, places, and events portrayed in this work are either products of the author's imagination or used fictitiously.

SEASONS OF GLASS AND IRON

Copyright © 2026 by Amal El-Mohtar

All rights reserved.

A Tordotcom Book
Published by Tom Doherty Associates / Tor Publishing Group
120 Broadway
New York, NY 10271

www.torpublishinggroup.com

Tor® is a registered trademark of Macmillan Publishing Group, LLC.

EU Representative: Macmillan Publishers Ireland Ltd, 1st Floor, The Liffey Trust Centre, 117–126 Sheriff Street Upper, Dublin 1, D01 YC43

The Library of Congress Cataloging-in-Publication Data is available upon request.

ISBN 978-1-250-34100-6 (hardcover)
ISBN 978-1-250-34101-3 (ebook)

The publisher of this book does not authorize the use or reproduction of any part of this book in any manner for the purpose of training artificial intelligence technologies or systems. The publisher of this book expressly reserves this book from the Text and Data Mining exception in accordance with Article 4(3) of the European Union Digital Single Market Directive 2019/790.

Our books may be purchased in bulk for specialty retail/wholesale, literacy, corporate/premium, educational, and subscription box use. Please contact MacmillanSpecialMarkets@macmillan.com.

First Edition: 2026

Printed in the United States of America

10 9 8 7 6 5 4 3 2 1

*For my parents,
Leila and Oussama,
who've loved me through all seasons.*

CONTENTS

Introduction	1
Seasons of Glass and Iron	5
The Green Book	22
Madeleine	31
The Lonely Sea in the Sky	47
Song for an Ancient City	60
And Their Lips Rang with the Sun	64
A Tale of Ash in Seven Birds	77
Qahr	82
The Truth About Owls	86
Wing	100
A Hollow Play	104
Thunderstorm in Glasgow, July 25, 2013	125
Anabasis	127
To Follow the Waves	130
Pieces	146
John Hollowback and the Witch	148
Florilegia; or, Some Lies About Flowers	169
Pockets	185

SEASONS
OF GLASS
AND IRON

INTRODUCTION

The years during which I wrote the stories and poems in this collection overlapped significantly with the years I spent studying British literature of the eighteenth and nineteenth centuries. A common feature of these periods' works is the Author's Preface. Taken at face value, the preface is often an apology, a humble obeisance made for the affront of taking up space—between covers, on a shelf, in the public eye. But the preface can also be wry and arch, or it can be a stiff, resentful performance—a dogged assertion of having earned the right to the audacity of authorship.[*]

As of this paragraph, I haven't entirely settled on which this will be.[†]

With all love and respect to the traditional front matter of the past, if I were to wax apologetic here it would be for not taking up more space—this introduction is the only thing I've written specifically for this collection. What I *do* take up is time: everything gathered here was first published in a magazine or anthology or on the public internet more generally between 2008 and 2023.

Fifteen years is a lot of time to be generous towards. I was twenty-three in 2008; I'm forty now. There are stories here that grew out of relationships that have since ended: with friends, with magazines, with universities. There are stories that I re-read with a telescoping memory: recalling where I was and what I was doing while clothing incidents from my earliest childhood in the confident wisdom of my mid-twenties. Threaded through all of them is a secret history of internets: the internet of LiveJournal and blog

---

[*] Or it can be outright fabrication: Horace Walpole wrote two Prefaces to *The Castle of Otranto* (1764), the first asserting that he was merely translating an authentic Italian text dated to 1529, and the second apologizing to his readers for the ruse.
[†] Probably not a fabrication! Although you'll have to wait for the second edition to find out.

posts and desktop computers (2006–2014), and later the internet of Twitter and mobile phones (2014–2022). Some stories have had surprising afterlives: reprints, awards, getting translated into other languages, or, most notably to me, performed by LeVar Burton, one of my childhood heroes. Every story has a story, and I find myself resisting the urge to treat the collection like a photo album, pointing to each snapshot to say *this is from when I was living in Cornwall and listening to a lot of Patrick Wolf,* or *this is from when I first learned about settler-colonialism.*

A fellow author once told me they thought a short story collection should make "a coherent aesthetic argument," which impressed me enough that I've repeated it to students over the years. But of the eighteen pieces here, eleven were commissioned for specific projects, usually with some core thematic (witches, steampunk, fairy tales) or demographic (Arab, women, queer) concern. I wasn't sure what argument, coherent or otherwise, would emerge from gathering my favourites, and I was curious to see if they'd make a pattern, surface something deep about myself.

Mostly, what emerged is that I love women.

I love women talking to each other. I love women reading each other, through letters and journals and flowers, offering up the stories of themselves to each other's tender scrutiny. I love women being friends and being lovers, in all of their shapes, across the breadth and depth of their lives. Over and over, in these stories, I find myself returning to what Emily Yoshida called "the terrifying magic of two women in a room, talking," and agreeing that "there's still so much of it we haven't explored yet."[*]

This in and of itself doesn't come as a surprise to me—several of these pieces emerged from conversations with dear friends, and were often the result of very deliberately wanting to centre and honour them, as an assertion of the truth of my own life against the narratives I most commonly received. But the sheer consistency of it, the insistence on it, was reassuring to encounter—to find myself,

---

[*] Emily Yoshida, "What Persona Is Still Teaching Us About Women Onscreen, 50 Years Later," Vulture, May 12, 2017.

year on year, recommitting to my love for women even as every generation upcycles new, more fashionable ways to hate them.*

Writing an introduction for another author's work is an honour, a pleasure, an invitation to run one's fingers over the topography of their oeuvre and admire its hills and valleys. Writing an introduction to one's own is a matter of choosing a stance. Ultimately I love these stories and poems, these earnest time capsules of my younger selves striving out in pursuit of friendship and belonging, certain that a better world would be just over the horizon if they could only find the words to shape it into being—if they could read this world we live in hard enough against its grain to carve from it some fundamental truths.

I'm grateful for the opportunity to collect them here, to offer you this small banquet of years, these seasons of glass and iron.

---

* Another common type of preface from days past is an apology for writing while being a woman: either explicitly, with a focus on the achievements that might justify the endeavour, or implicitly, with the device of a man's name.

SEASONS OF GLASS
AND IRON

For Lara West

Tabitha walks, and thinks of shoes.

She has been thinking about shoes for a very long time: the length of three and a half pairs, to be precise, though it's hard to reckon in iron. Easier to reckon how many pairs are left: of the seven she set out with, three remain, strapped securely against the outside of the pack she carries, weighing it down. The seasons won't keep still, slip past her with the landscape, so she can't say for certain whether a year of walking wears out a sole, but it seems about right. She always means to count the steps, starting with the next pair, but it's easy to get distracted.

She thinks about shoes because she cannot move forward otherwise: Each iron strap cuts, rubs, bruises, blisters, and her pain fuels their ability to cross rivers, mountains, airy breaches between cliffs. She must move forward, or the shoes will never be worn down. The shoes must be worn down.

It's always hard to strap on a new pair.

Three pairs of shoes ago, she was in a pine forest, and the sharp green smell of it woke something in her, something that was more than numbness, numbers. (*Number? I hardly know 'er!* She'd laughed for a week, off and on, at her little joke.) She shivered in the needled light, bundled her arms into her fur cloak but stretched her toes into the autumn earth, and wept to feel, for a moment, something like free—before the numbers crept in with the cold, and *one down, six to go* found its way into her relief that it was, in fact, possible to get through a single pair in a lifetime.

Two pairs of shoes ago, she was in the middle of a lake, striding across the deep blue of it, when the last scrap of sole gave way.

She collapsed and floundered as she undid the straps, scrambled to pull the next pair off her pack, sank until she broke a toe in jamming them on, then found herself on the surface again, limping toward the far shore.

One pair of shoes ago, she was by the sea. She soaked her feet in salt and stared up at the stars and wondered whether drowning would hurt.

She recalls shoes her brothers have worn: a pair of seven-league boots, tooled in soft leather; winged sandals; satin slippers that turned one invisible. How strange, she thinks, that her brothers had shoes that lightened their steps and tightened the world, made it small and easy to explore, discover.

Perhaps, she thinks, it isn't strange at all: Why shouldn't shoes help their wearers travel? Perhaps, she thinks, what's strange is the shoes women are made to wear: shoes of glass; shoes of paper; shoes of iron heated red-hot; shoes to dance to death in.

How strange, she thinks, and walks.

⁓

Amira makes an art of stillness.

She sits atop a high glass hill, its summit shaped into a throne of sorts, thick and smooth, perfectly suited to her so long as she does not move. Magic girdles her, roots her stillness through the throne. She has weathered storms here, the sleek-fingered rain glistening between glass and gown, hair and skin, seeking to shift her this way or that—but she has held herself straight, upright, a golden apple in her lap.

She is sometimes hungry, but the magic looks after that; she is often tired, and the magic encourages sleep. The magic keeps her brown skin from burning during the day, and keeps her silk-shod feet from freezing at night—so long as she is still, so long as she keeps her glass seat atop her glass hill.

From her vantage point she can see a great deal: farmers working their land; travelers walking from village to village; the occasional robbery or murder. There is much she would like to come down from her hill and tell people, but for the suitors.

Clustered and clamouring around the bottom of her glass hill are the knights, princes, shepherds' lads who have fallen violently in love with her. They shout encouragement to one another as they ride their warhorses up the glass hill, breaking against it in wave after wave, reaching for her.

As they slide down the hill, their horses foaming, legs twisted or shattered, they scream curses at her: the cunt, the witch, can't she see what she's doing to them, glass whore on a glass hill, they'll get her tomorrow, tomorrow, tomorrow.

Amira grips her golden apple. By day she distracts herself with birds: all the wild geese who fly overhead, the gulls and swifts and swallows, the larks. She remembers a story about nettle shirts thrown up to swans, and wonders if she could reach up and pluck a feather from them to give herself wings.

By night, she strings shapes around the stars, imagines familiar constellations into difference: suppose the great ladle was a sickle instead, or a bear?

When she runs out of birds and stars, she remembers that she chose this.

༄

Tabitha first sees the glass hill as a knife's edge of light, scything a green swathe across her vision before she can look away. She is stepping out of a forest; the morning sun is vicious, bright with no heat in it; the frosted grass crunches under the press of her iron heels, but some of it melts cold relief against the skin exposed through the straps.

She sits at the forest's edge and watches the light change.

There are men at the base of the hill; their noise is a dull ringing that reminds her of the ocean. She watches them spur their horses into bleeding. Strong magic in that hill, she thinks, to make men behave so foolishly; strong magic in that hill to withstand so many iron hooves.

She looks down at her own feet, then up at the hill. She reckons the quality of her pain in numbers, but not by degree: If her pain is a six it is because it is cold, blue with an edge to it; if her pain is a seven it is red, inflamed, bleeding; if her pain is a three it has a rounded yellow feel, dull and perhaps draining infection.

Her pain at present is a five, green and brown, sturdy and stable, and ought to be enough to manage the ascent.

She waits until sunset, and sets out across the clearing.

⁓

Amira watches a mist rise as the sun sets, and her heart sings to see everything made so soft: a great cool *hush* over all, a smell of water with no stink in it, no blood or sweat. She loves to see the world so vanished, so quiet, so calm.

Her heart skips a beat when she hears the scraping, somewhere beneath her, somewhere within the mist: a grinding, scouring sort of noise, steady as her nerves aren't, because something is climbing the glass hill and this isn't how it was supposed to work, no one is supposed to be able to reach her, but magic is magic is magic and there is always stronger magic—

She thinks it is a bear, at first, then sees it is a furred hood, glimpses a pale delicate chin beneath it, a wide mouth twisted into a teeth-gritting snarl from the effort of the climb.

Amira stares, uncertain, as the hooded, horseless stranger reaches the top, and stops, and stoops, and pants, and sheds the warm weight of the fur. Amira sees a woman, and the woman sees her, and the woman looks like a feather and a sword and very, very hungry.

Amira offers up her golden apple without a word.

⁓

Tabitha had thought the woman in front of her a statue, a copper ornament, an idol, until her arm moved. Some part of her feels she should pause before accepting food from a magical woman on a glass hill, but it's dwarfed by a ravenousness she's not felt in weeks; in the shoes, she mostly forgets about her stomach until weakness threatens to prevent her from putting one foot in front of the other.

The apple doesn't look like food, but she bites into it, and the skin breaks like burnt sugar, the flesh drips clear, sweet juice. She eats it, core and all, before looking at the woman on the throne again and saying—with a gruffness she does not feel or intend—"Thank you."

"My name is Amira," says the woman, and Tabitha marvels at how she speaks without moving any other part of her body, how measured are the mechanics of her mouth. "Have you come to marry me?"

Tabitha stares. She wipes the juice from her chin, as if that could erase the golden apple from her belly. "Do I have to?"

Amira blinks. "No. Only—that's why people try to climb the hill, you know."

"Oh. No, I just—" Tabitha coughs, slightly, embarrassed. "I'm just passing through."

Silence.

"The mist was thick, I got turned around—"

"You climbed"—Amira's voice is very quiet—"a glass hill"—and even—"by accident?"

Tabitha fidgets with the hem of her shirt.

"Well," says Amira, "it's nice to meet you, ah—"

"Tabitha."

"Yes. Very nice to meet you, Tabitha."

Further silence. Tabitha chews her bottom lip while looking down into the darkness at the base of the hill. Then, quietly: "Why are you even up here?"

Amira looks at her coolly. "By accident."

Tabitha snorts. "I see. Very well. Look." Tabitha points to her iron-strapped feet. "I have to wear down the shoes. They're magic. I have a notion that the stranger the surface—the harder it would be to walk on something usually—the faster the sole diminishes. So your magical hill here . . ."

Amira nods, or at least it seems to Tabitha that she nods—it may have been more of a lengthened blink that conveyed the impression of her head's movement.

". . . it seemed like just the thing. I didn't know there was anyone at the top, though; I waited until the men at the bottom had left, as they seemed a nasty lot—"

It isn't that Amira shivers, but that the quality of her stillness grows denser. Tabitha feels something like alarm beginning a dull ring in her belly.

"They leave as the nights turn colder. You're more than welcome to stay," says Amira, in tones of deepest courtesy, "and scrape your shoes against the glass."

Tabitha nods, and stays, because somewhere within the measured music of Amira's words she hears *please*.

Amira feels half-asleep, sitting and speaking with someone who isn't about to destroy her, break her apart for the half kingdom inside.

"Have they placed you up here?" Tabitha asks, and Amira finds it strange to hear anger that isn't directed at her, anger that seems at her service.

"No," she says softly. "I chose this." Then, before Tabitha can say anything else, "Why do you walk in iron shoes?"

Tabitha's mouth is open but her words are stopped up, and Amira can see them changing direction like a flock of starlings in her throat. She decides to change the subject.

"Have you ever heard the sound geese make when they fly overhead? I don't mean the honking, everyone hears that, but—their wings. Have you ever heard the sound of their wings?"

Tabitha smiles a little. "Like thunder, when they take off from a river."

"What? Oh." A pause; Amira has never seen a river. "No—it's nothing like that when they fly above you. It's . . . a creaking, like a stove door with no squeak in it, as if the geese are machines dressed in flesh and feathers. It's a beautiful sound—beneath the honking it's a low drone, but if they're flying quietly, it's like . . . clothing, somehow, like if you listened just right, you might find yourself wearing wings."

Without noticing, Amira has closed her eyes while speaking of the geese; she opens them to see Tabitha looking at her with curious focus, and feels briefly disoriented by the scrutiny. She isn't used to being listened to.

"If we're lucky," she says softly, turning a golden apple around and around in her hands, "we'll hear some tonight. It's the right time of year."

⸻

Tabitha opens her mouth, then shuts it so hard her back teeth meet. She does not ask *how long have you been sitting here, that you know when to expect the geese;* she does not ask *where did that golden apple come from? Didn't I just eat it?* She understands what Amira is doing and is grateful; she does not want to talk about the shoes.

"I've never heard that sound," she says instead, slowly, trying not to look at the apple. "But I've seen them on rivers and lakes. Hundreds at a time, clamouring like old wives at a well, until something startles them into rising, and then it's like drums, or thunder, or a storm of winds through branches. An enormous sound, almost deafening—not one to listen closely for."

"I would love to hear that," Amira whispers, looking out toward the woods. "To see them. What do they look like?"

"Thick, dark—" Tabitha reaches for words. "Like the river itself is rising, lifting its skirts and taking off."

Amira smiles, and Tabitha feels a tangled warmth in her chest at the thought of having given her something.

⸻

"Would you like another apple?" offers Amira, and notes the wariness in Tabitha's eye. "They keep coming back. I eat them myself from time to time. I wasn't sure if—I thought it was meant as a prize for whoever climbed the hill, but I suppose the notion is they don't go away unless I give them to a man."

Tabitha frowns, but accepts. As she eats, Amira feels Tabitha's eyes on her empty hands, waiting to catch the apple's reappearance, and tries not to smile—she'd done as much herself the first fifty or so times, testing the magic for loopholes. Novel, however, to watch someone watching for the apple.

As Tabitha nears the last bite, Amira sees her look confused, distracted, as if by a hair on her tongue or an unfamiliar smell—and then the apple's in Amira's hands again, feeling for all the world like it never left.

"I don't think the magic lets us see it happen," says Amira, almost by way of apology for Tabitha's evident disappointment. "But so long as I sit here, I have one."

"I'd like to try that again," says Tabitha, and Amira smiles.

⁓

First, Tabitha waits. She counts the seconds, watching Amira's empty hands. After seven hundred seconds, there is an apple in Amira's hand. Amira stares at it, looking from it to the one in Tabitha's.

"That's . . . never happened before. I didn't think there could be more than one at a time."

Tabitha takes the second apple from her but bites into it, counting the mouthfuls slowly, watching Amira's hands the while. After the seventh bite, Amira's hands are full again. She hands the third apple over without a word.

Tabitha counts—the moments, the bites, the number of apples—until there are seven laid gleaming over the fur in her lap; when she takes an eighth from Amira, the first seven turn to sand.

"I think it's the magic on me," says Tabitha thoughtfully, dusting the apple sand out of her fur. "I'm bound in sevens—you're bound in ones. You can hold only one apple at a time—I can hold seven. Funny, isn't it?"

Amira's smile looks strained and vague, and only after a moment does Tabitha realize she's watching the wind-caught sand blowing off the hill.

⁓

Autumn crackles into winter, and frost rimes the glass hill into diamonds. By day, Amira watches fewer and fewer men slide down it while Tabitha sits by her, huddled into her fur; by night, Tabitha walks in slow circles around her as they talk about anything but glass and iron. While Tabitha walks, Amira looks more closely at her shackled feet, always glancing away before she can be drawn into staring. Through the sandal-like straps that wrap up to her ankle, Amira can see they are blackened, twisted ruins, toes bent at odd angles, scabbed and scarred.

One morning, Amira wakes to surprising warmth, and finds Tabitha's fur draped around her. She is so startled she almost rises from her seat to find her—has she left? Is she gone?—but Tabitha walks briskly back into her line of sight before Amira can do anything drastic, rubbing her thin arms, blowing on her fingers. Amira is aghast.

"Why did you give me your cloak? Take it back!"

"Your lips were turning blue in your sleep, and you can't *move*—"

"It's all right, Tabitha, please—" The desperation in Amira's voice stops Tabitha's circling, pins her in place. Reluctantly, she takes her fur back, draws it over her own shoulders again. "The apples—or the hill itself, I'm not sure—keep me warm enough. Here, have another."

Tabitha appears unconvinced. "But you looked so cold—"

"Perhaps it's like your feet," says Amira, before she can stop herself. "They look broken, but you can still walk on them."

༄

Tabitha stares at her for a long moment, before accepting the apple. "They feel broken too. Although"—shifting her gaze to the apple, lowering her voice—"less and less, lately."

She takes a bite. While she eats, Amira ventures, quietly, "I thought you'd left."

Tabitha raises an eyebrow, swallows, and chuckles. "Without my cloak, in winter? I like you, Amira, but—" *Not that much* dies on her tongue, as she tastes the lie in it. She coughs. "That would be silly. Anyway, I wouldn't leave you without saying good-bye." An uncertain pause then. "Though, if you tire of company—"

"No," says Amira, swiftly, surely. "No."

༄

Snow falls, and the last of the suitors abandon their camps, grumbling home. Tabitha walks her circles around Amira's throne by day now as well as night, unafraid of being seen.

"They won't be back until spring," says Amira, smiling. "Though then they keep their efforts up well into the night as the days get longer. Perhaps to make up for lost time."

Tabitha frowns, and something in the circle of their talk tightens enough for her to ask, as she walks, "How many winters have you spent up here?"

Amira shrugs. "Three, I think. How many winters have you spent in those shoes?"

"This is their first," says Tabitha, pausing. "But there were three pairs before this one."

"Ah. Is this the last?"

Tabitha chuckles. "No. Seven in all. And I'm only halfway through this one."

Amira nods. "Perhaps, come spring, you'll have finished it."

"Perhaps," says Tabitha, before beginning her circuit again.

༄

Winter thaws, and everything smells of snowmelt and wet wood. Tabitha ventures down the glass hill and brings Amira snowdrops, twining them into her dark hair. "They look like stars," murmurs Tabitha, and something in Amira creaks and snaps like ice on a bough.

"Tabitha," she says, "it's almost spring."

"Mm," says Tabitha, intent on a tricky braid.

"I'd like—" Amira draws a deep, quiet breath. "I'd like to tell you a story."

Tabitha pauses—then, resuming her braiding, says, "I'd like to hear one."

"I don't know if I'm any good at telling stories," Amira adds, turning a golden apple over and over in her hands, "but that's no reason not to try."

༄

Once upon a time there was a rich king who had no sons, and whose only daughter was too beautiful. She was so beautiful that men could not stop themselves from reaching out to touch her in corridors or following her to her rooms, so beautiful that words of desire tumbled from men's lips like diamonds and toads, irresistible and unstoppable. The king took pity on these men and drew his daughter aside, saying, Daughter, only a husband can break the spell over these men; only a husband can prevent them from behaving so gallantly toward you.

When the king's daughter suggested a ball, that these men might find husbands for themselves and so be civilized, the king was not amused. You must be wed, said the king, before some guard cannot but help himself to your virtue.

The king's daughter was afraid, and said, Suppose you sent me away?

No, said the king, for how should I keep an eye on you then?

The king's daughter, who did not want a husband, said, Suppose you chose a neighbouring prince for me?

Impossible, said the king, for you are my only daughter, and I cannot favour one neighbour over another; the balance of power is precarious and complicated.

The king's daughter read an unspeakable conclusion in her father's eye, and in a rush to keep it from reaching his mouth, said, Suppose you placed me atop a glass hill where none could reach me, and say that only the man who can ride up the hill in full armour may claim me as his bride?

But that is an impossible task, said the king, looking thoughtful.

Then you may keep your kingdom whole, and your eye on me, and men safe from me, said his daughter.

It was done just as she said, and by her will. And if she's not gone, she lives there still.

When Amira stops speaking, she is taken aback to feel Tabitha scowling at her.

"That," growls Tabitha, "is *absurd*."

Amira blinks. She had expected, she realizes, some sympathy, some understanding. "Oh?"

"What father seeks to protect men from their pursuit of his daughter? As well seek to protect the wolf from the rabbit!"

"I am not a rabbit," says Amira, though Tabitha, who has dropped her hair and is pacing, incensed, continues.

"How could it be your fault that men are loutish and ill-mannered? Amira, I promise you, if your hair were straw and your face dull as dishwater, men—bad men—would still behave this way. Do you think the suitors around the hill can see what you look like, all the way up here?"

Amira keeps quiet, unsure what to say—she wonders why she wants to apologize with one side of her mouth and defend herself with the other.

"You said you *chose* this," Tabitha spits. "What manner of choice was that? A wolf's maw or a glass hill."

"On the hill," says Amira, lips tight, "I want for nothing. I do not need food or drink or shelter. No one can touch me. That's all I ever wanted—for no one to be able to touch me. So long as I sit here, and eat apples, and do not move, I have everything I want."

Tabitha is silent for a moment. Then, more gently than before, she says, "I thought you wanted to see a river full of geese."

Amira says nothing.

Tabitha says, still more gently, "Mine are not the only iron shoes in the world."

Still nothing. Amira's heart grinds within her, until Tabitha sighs.

"Let me tell you a story about iron shoes."

Once upon a time, a woman fell in love with a bear. She didn't mean to; it was only that he was both fearsome and kind to her, that he was dangerous and clever and could teach her about hunting salmon and harvesting wild honey, and she had been lonely for a long time. She felt special with his eyes on her, for what other woman could say she was loved by a bear without being torn between his teeth? She loved him for loving her as he loved no one else.

They were wed, and at night the bear put on a man's shape to share her bed in the dark. At first he was gentle and kind, and the woman was happy; but in time the bear began to change—not his shape, which she knew as well as her own, but his manner. He grew bitter and jealous, accused her of longing for a bear who was a man day and night. He said she was a terrible wife who knew nothing of how to please bears. By day he spoke to her in a language of thorns and claws, and by night he hurt her with his body. It was hard for the woman to endure, but how can one love a bear entirely without pain? She only worked harder to please him.

In the seventh year of their marriage, the woman begged her husband to allow her to go visit her family. He consented to her departure on the condition that she not be alone with her mother, for surely her mother would poison her against him. She promised—but the woman's mother saw the marks on her, the bruises and scratches, and hurried her into a room alone. In a moment of weakness, the woman listened to her mother's words against her husband, calling him a monster, a demon. Her mother insisted that she leave him—but how could she? He was still her own dear husband in spite of it all—she only wished him to be as he had been when she first married him. Perhaps he was under a curse, after all, and only she could lift it?

Burn his bear skin, said her mother. Perhaps that is his curse. Perhaps he longs to be a man day and night but is forbidden to say so.

When she returned to her husband, he seemed to have missed her, and was kind and sweet with her. In the night while he slept next to her in his man's shape, she gathered up his bear skin as quietly as she could, built up the fire, and threw it in.

The skin did not burn. But it began to scream.

It woke her husband, who flew into a great rage, saying she had broken her promise to him. When the woman wept that she had only wanted to free him from his curse, he picked up the skin, tossed it over her shoulders, and threw a bag of iron shoes at her feet. He said that the only way to make him a man day and night was to wear his bear's skin while wearing out seven pairs of iron shoes, one for each year of their marriage.

So she set out to do so.

Amira's eyes are wide and rimmed in red, and Tabitha flushes, picks at a burr caught in her husband's fur.

"I knew marriage was monstrous," says Amira, "but I never imagined—"

Tabitha shrugs. "It wasn't all bad. And I broke my promise—if I hadn't seen my mother, I would never have thought to try and burn the skin. Promises are important to bears. This, here"—she gestures at the glass hill—"*this* is monstrous: to keep you prisoner, to prevent you from moving or speaking out—"

"Your husband wanted to keep you from speaking! To your *mother!*"

"And look what happened when I did," says Tabitha stiffly. "It was a test of loyalty, and I failed it. You did *nothing wrong*."

"That's funny," says Amira, unsmiling, "because to me, every day feels like a test: Will I move from this hill or not, will I grasp at a bird or not, will I toss an apple down to a man when I shouldn't, will I speak too loudly, will I give them a reason to hurt me and fall off the hill, and every day I don't is a day I pass—"

"That's different. That's dreadful."

"I don't see the difference!"

"You don't *love* this hill!"

"I love you," says Amira, very softly. "I love you, and I do not understand how someone who loves you would want to hurt you, or make you walk in iron shoes."

Tabitha chews her lips, trying to shape words from them, and fails.

"I told my story poorly," she says, finally. "I told it selfishly. I did not speak of how good he was—how he made me laugh, the things he taught me. I could live in the iron shoes because of his guidance, because of knowing the poison berry from the pure, because he taught me to hunt. What happened to him, the change in him"— Tabitha feels very tired—"it must have had to do with me. I was meant to endure it until the curse broke, and I failed. It's the only thing that makes sense."

༄

Amira looks at Tabitha's ruined feet.

"Do you truly believe," she says, with all the care she pours into keeping her spine taut and straight on her glass seat, "that I had nothing to do with those men's attentions? That they would have behaved that way no matter what I looked like?"

"Yes," says Tabitha firmly.

"Then is it not possible"—hesitant, now, to even speak the thought—"that your husband's cruelty had nothing to do with you? That it had nothing to do with a curse? You said he hurt you in both his shapes."

"But I—"

"If you've worn your shoes halfway down, shouldn't you be bending your steps toward him again, that the last pair be destroyed near the home you shared?"

In the shifting light of the moon both their faces have a bluish cast, but Amira sees Tabitha's go gray.

"When I was a girl," says Tabitha thickly, as if working around something in her throat, "I dreamt of marriage as a golden thread between hearts—a ribbon binding one to the other, warm as a day in summer. I did not dream a chain of iron shoes."

"Tabitha"—and Amira does not know what to do except to reach for her hand, clutch it, look at her in the way she looks at the geese, longing to speak and be understood—"you did nothing wrong."

Tabitha holds Amira's gaze. "Neither did you."

They stay that way for a long time, until the sound of seven geese's beating wings startles them into looking up at the stars.

⌒

The days and nights grow warmer; more and more geese fly overhead. One morning, as Tabitha walks her circle around Amira, she stumbles, trips, and falls forward into Amira's arms.

"Are you all right?" Amira whispers, while Tabitha clutches at the throne, shaking her head, suddenly unsteady.

"The shoes," she says, marvelling. "They're finished. The fourth pair. Amira." Tabitha laughs, surprises herself to hear it sound more like a sob. "They're done."

Amira smiles at her, bends forward to kiss her forehead. "Congratulations," she murmurs, and Tabitha hears much more than the word as she reaches, shaky, wobbling, for the next pair in her pack.

"Wait," says Amira quietly, and Tabitha pauses. "Wait. Please. Don't—" Amira bites her lip, looks away. "You don't have to—you can stay here without—"

Tabitha understands, and returns her hand to Amira's. "I can't stay up here forever. I have to leave before the suitors come back."

Amira draws a deep breath. "I know."

"I've had a thought, though."

"Oh?" Amira smiles softly. "Do you want to marry me after all?"

"Yes."

Amira's stillness turns crystalline in her surprise.

⁓

Tabitha is talking, and Amira can barely understand it, feels Tabitha's words slipping off her mind like sand off a glass hill. Anything, anything to keep her from putting her feet back in those iron cages—

"I mean—not as a husband would. But to take you away from here. If you want. Before your suitors return. Can I do that?"

Amira looks at the golden apple in her hand. "I don't know—where would we go?"

"Anywhere! The shoes can walk anywhere, over anything—"

"Back to your husband?"

Something like a thunderclap crosses Tabitha's face. "No. Not there."

Amira looks up. "If we are to marry, I insist on an exchange of gifts. Leave the fur and the shoes behind."

"But—"

"I know what they cost you. I don't want to walk on air and darkness if the price is your pain."

"Amira," says Tabitha helplessly, "I don't think I can walk without them anymore."

"Have you tried? You've been eating golden apples a long while. And you can lean on me."

"But—they might be useful—"

"The glass hill has been very useful to me," says Amira quietly, "and the golden apples have kept me warm and whole and fed. But I will leave them—I will follow you into woods and across fields, I will be hungry and cold and my feet will hurt. But if you are with me, Tabitha, then I will learn to hunt and fish and tell the poison berry from the pure, and I will see a river raise its skirt of geese, and listen to them make a sound like thunder. Do you believe I can do this?"

"Yes," says Tabitha, a choking in her voice, "yes, I do."

"I believe you can walk without iron shoes. Leave them here—and in exchange, I will give you my shoes of silk, and we will fill your pack with seven golden apples, and if you eat from them sparingly, perhaps they will help you walk until we can find you something better."

"But we can't climb down the hill without a pair of shoes!"

"We don't need to." Amira smiles, stroking Tabitha's hair. "Falling's easy—it's keeping still that's hard."

Neither says anything for a time. Then—carefully, on her knees, for the hill is slippery to her now—Tabitha sheds her fur cloak, unstraps the iron shoes from her feet, and gives them and her pack to Amira. Amira removes the three remaining pairs and replaces them with apples, drawing the pack's straps tight over the seventh. She passes the pack back to Tabitha, who shoulders it.

Then, taking Tabitha's hands in hers, Amira breathes deep and stands up.

The glass throne cracks. There is a sound like hard rain, a roar of whispers as the glass hill shivers into sand. It swallows fur and shoes; it swallows Amira and Tabitha together; it settles into a dome-shaped dune with a final hiss.

Hands still clasped, Amira and Tabitha tumble out of it together, coughing, laughing, shaking sand from their hair and skin. They stand, and wait, and no golden apple appears to part their hands from each other.

"Where should we go?" whispers one to the other.

"Away," she replies, and holding on to each other, they stumble into the spring, the wide world rising to meet them with the dawn.

THE GREEN BOOK

MS. Orre. 1013A Miscellany of materials copied from within Master Leuwin Orrerel's (*d.* Lady Year 673, Bright Be the Edges) library by Dominic Merrowin (*d.* Lady Year 673, Bright Be the Edges). Contains Acts I and II of Aster's *The Golden Boy's Last Ship*, Act III scene I of *The Rose Petal*, and the entirety of *The Blasted Oak*. Incomplete copy of item titled only THE GREEN BOOK, authorship multiple and uncertain. Notable for extensive personal note by Merrowin, intended as correspondence with unknown recipient, detailing evidence of personal connection between Orrerel and the Sisterhood of Knives. Many leaves regrettably lost, especially within text of THE GREEN BOOK: evidence of discussion of Lady Year religious and occult philosophies, traditions in the musical education of second daughters, and complex receptions of Aster's poetry, all decayed beyond recovery. Markers placed at sites of likely omission.

My dear friend,

I am copying this out while I can. Leuwin is away, has left me in charge of the library. He has been doing that more and more, lately—errands for the Sisterhood, he says, but I know it's mostly his own mad research. Now I know why.

His mind is disturbed. Twelve years of teaching me, and he never once denied me the reading of any book, but this—this thing has hold of him, I am certain plays with him. I thought it was his journal, at first; he used to write in it so often, closet himself with it for hours, and it seemed to bring him joy. Now I feel there is something fell and chanty about it, and beg your opinion of the whole, that we may work together to Leuwin's salvation.

The book I am copying out is small—only four inches by five. It is a vivid green, quite exactly the colour of sunlight through the oak leaves in the arbour, and just as mottled; its cover is pulp wrapped in paper, and its pages are thick with needle-thorn and something that smells of thyme.

There are six different hands in evidence. The first, the invocation, is archaic: large block letters with hardly any ornamentation. I place it during Journey Year 200–250, Long Did It Wind, and it is written almost in green paste: I observe a grainy texture to the letters, though I dare not touch them. Sometimes the green of them is obscured by rust-brown stains that I suppose to be blood, given the circumstances that produced the second hand.

The second hand is modern, as are the rest, though they vary significantly from each other.

The second hand shows evidence of fluency, practice, and ease in writing, though the context was no doubt grim. It is written in heavy charcoal, and is much faded, but still legible.

The third hand is a child's uncertain wobbling, where the letters are large and uneven; it is written in fine ink with a heavy implement. I find myself wondering if it was a knife.

The fourth is smooth, an agony of right-slanted whorls and loops, a gallows-cursive that nooses my throat with the thought of who must have written it.

The fifth hand is very similar to the second. It is dramatically improved, but there is no question that it was produced by the same individual, who claims to be named Cynthia. It is written in ink rather than charcoal—but the ink is strange. There is no trace of nib or quill in the letters. It is as if they welled up from within the page.

The sixth hand is Leuwin's.

I am trying to copy them as exactly as possible, and am bracketing my own additions.

Go in Gold,
Dominic Merrowin

[First Hand: invocation]
Hail!
To the Mistress of Crossroads, **[blood stain to far right]**

The Fetch in the Forest
The Witch of the Glen
The Hue and Cry of mortal men
Winsome and lissom and Fey!
Hail to the **[blood stain obscuring]** Mother of Changelings
of doubled paths and trebled means
of troubled dreams and salt and ash
Hail!

[Second Hand: charcoal smudging, two pages; dampened and stained]

Cold in here—death and shadows—funny there should be a book! the universe provides for last will and testament! **[illegible]**

[illegible] *I cannot write, mustn't* **[illegible]** *they're coming I hear them they'll hear scratching* **[illegible]** *knives to tickle my throat oh please*

They say they're kind. I think that's what we tell ourselves to be less afraid because how could anyone know? Do **[blood stain]** *the dead speak?*

Do the tongues blackening around their necks sing?

why do I write? save me, please, save me, stone and ivy and bone I want to live I want to breathe they have no right **[illegible]**

[Third Hand: Chaotic, uneven. Implement uncertain— possibly a knife, ink-tipped]

What a beautiful book this is. I wonder where she found it. I could write poems in it. This paper is so thick, so creamy, it puts me in mind of the bones in the ivy. Her bones were lovely! I cannot wait to see how they will sprout in it—I kept her zygomatic bone, but her lacrimal bits will make such pretty patterns in the leaves!

I could almost feel that any trace of ink against this paper would be a poem, would comfort my lack of skill.

I must show my sisters. I wish I had more of this paper to give them. We could write each other such secrets as only bones ground into pulpy paper could know. Or I would write of how beautiful are sister-green's eyes, how shy are sister-salt's lips, how golden sister-bell's laugh

[Fourth Hand: cursive, right-slanted; high-quality ink, smooth and fine]

Strange, how it will not burn, how its pages won't tear. Strange that there is such pleasure in streaking ink along the cream of it; this paper makes me want to touch my lips. Pretty thing, you have been tricksy, tempting my little Sisters into spilling secrets.

There is strong magic here. Perhaps Master Leuwin in his tower would appreciate such a curiosity. Strange that I write in it, then—strange magic. Leuwin, you have my leave to laugh when you read this. Perhaps you will write to me anon of its history before that unfortunate girl and my wayward Sister scribbled in it.

That is, if I send it to you. Its charm is powerful—I may wish to study it further, see if we mightn't steep it in elderflower wine and discover what tincture results.

[Fifth Hand: strange ink; no evidence of implement; style resembles Second Hand very closely]

Hello?
Where am I?
Please, someone speak to me
Oh
Oh no

[Sixth Hand: Master Leuwin Orrerel]

I will speak to you. Hello.

I think I see what happened, and I see that you see. I am sorry for you. But I think it would be best if you tried to sleep. I will shut the green over the black and you must think of sinking into sweetness, think of dreaming to fly. Think of echoes, and songs. Think of fragrant tea and the stars. No one can harm you now, little one. I will hide you between two great leather tomes—

[Fifth Hand—alternating with Leuwin's hereafter]

Do you know Lady Aster?
Yes, of course.
Could you put me next to her, please? I love her plays.
I always preferred her poetry.

Her plays ARE poetry!
Of course, you're right. Next to her, then. What is your name?
Cynthia.
I am Master Leuwin.
I know. It's very kind of you to talk to me.
You're—**[ink blot]** forgive the ink blot, please. Does that hurt?
No more than poor penmanship ever does.
Leuwin? Are you there?
Yes. What can I do for you?
Speak to me, a little. Do you live alone?
Yes—well, except for Dominic, my student and apprentice. It is my intention to leave him this library one day—it is a library, you see, in a tower on a small hill, seven miles from the city of Leech—do you know it?
No. I've heard of it, though. Vicious monarchy, I heard.
I do not concern myself overmuch with politics. I keep records, that is all.
How lucky for you, to not have to concern yourself with politics. Records of what?
Everything I can. Knowledge. Learning. Curiosities. History and philosophy. Scientific advances, musical compositions and theory—some things I seek out, most are given to me by people who would have a thing preserved.
How ironic.
. . . Yes. Yes, I suppose it is, in your case.

[[DECAY, SEVERAL LEAVES LOST]]

Were you very beautiful, as a woman?
What woman would answer no, in my position?
An honest one.
I doubt I could have appeared more beautiful to you as a woman than as a book.
. . . Too honest.

[[DECAY, SEVERAL LEAVES LOST]]

What else is in your library?
Easier to ask what isn't! I am in pursuit of a book inlaid with mirrors—the text is so potent that it was written in reverse, and can only be read in reflection to prevent unwelcome effects.

Fascinating. Who wrote it?

I have a theory it was commissioned by a disgruntled professor, with a pun on "reflection" designed to shame his students into closer analyses of texts.

Hah! I hope that's the case. What else?

Oh, there is a history of the Elephant War written by a captain on the losing side, a codex from the Chrysanthemum Year (Bold Did It Bloom) about the seven uses of bone that the Sisterhood would like me to find, and

Cynthia I'm so sorry. Please, forgive me.

No matter. It isn't as if I've forgotten how I came to you in the first place, though you seem to quite frequently.

Why

Think VERY carefully about whether you want to ask this question, Leuwin.

Why did they kill you? . . . How did they?

Forbidden questions from their pet librarian? The world does turn. Do you really want to know?

Yes.

So do I. Perhaps you could ask them for me.

[[DECAY, SEVERAL LEAVES LOST]]

If I could find a way to get you out . . .

You and your ellipses. Was that supposed to be a question?

I might make it a quest.

I am dead, Leuwin. I have no body but this.

You have a voice. A mind.

I am a voice, a mind. I have nothing else.

Cynthia . . . What happens when we reach the end of this? When we run out of pages?

Endings do not differ overmuch from each other, I expect. Happy or sad, they are still endings.

Your ending had a rather surprising sequel.

True. Though I see it more as intermission—an interminable intermission, during which the actors have wandered home to get drunk.

[[DECAY, SEVERAL LEAVES LOST]]

Cynthia, I think I love you.

Cynthia?

Why don't you answer me?
Please, speak to me.
I'm tired, Leuwin.
I love you.
You love ink on a page. You don't lack for that here.
I love *you*.
Only because I speak to you. Only because no one but you reads these words. Only because I am the only book to be written to you, for you. Only because I allow you, in this small way, to be a book yourself.
I love you.
Stop.
Don't you love me?
Cynthia.
You can't lie, can you?
You can't lie, so you refuse to speak the truth.
I hate you.
Because you love me.
I hate you. Leave me alone.
I will write out Lady Aster's plays for you to read. I will write you her poetry. I will fill this with all that is beautiful in the world, for you, that you might live it.
Leuwin. No.
I will stop a few pages from the end, and you can read it over and over again, all the loveliest things . . .
Leuwin. No.
But I
STOP. I WANT TO LIVE. I WANT TO HOLD YOU AND FUCK YOU AND MAKE YOU TEA AND READ YOU PLAYS. I WANT YOU TO TOUCH MY CHEEK AND MY HAIR AND LOOK ME IN THE EYES WHEN YOU SAY YOU LOVE ME. I WANT TO LIVE!
And you, you want a woman in a book. You want to tremble over my binding and ruffle my pages and spill ink into me. No, I can't lie. Only the living can lie. I am dead. I am dead trees and dead horses boiled to glue. I hate you. Leave me alone.
[FINIS. Several blank pages remain]

You see he is mad.

I know he is looking for ways to extricate her from the book. I fear for him, in so deep with the Sisters—I fear for what he will ask of them—

Sweet Stars, there's more. I see it appearing as I write this—unnatural, chanty thing! I shall not reply. I must not reply, lest I fall into her trap as he did! But I will write this for you—I am committed to completeness.

Following immediately after the last, then:

Dominic, why are you doing this?

You won't answer me? Fair enough.

I can feel when I am being read, Dominic. It's a beautiful feeling, in some ways—have you ever felt beautiful? Sometimes I think only people who are not beautiful can feel so, can feel the shape of the exception settling on them like a mantle, like a morning mist.

Being read is like feeling beautiful, knowing your hair to be just-so and your clothing to be well-put-together and your colour to be high and bright, and to feel, in the moment of beauty, that you are being observed.

The world shifts. You pretend not to see that you are being admired, desired. You think about whether or not to play the game of glances, and you smile to yourself, and you know the person has seen your smile, and it was beautiful, too. Slowly, you become aware of how they see you, and without looking, quite, you know that they are playing the game too, that they imagine you seeing them as beautiful, and it is a splendid game, truly.

Leuwin reads me quite often, without saying anything further to me. I ache when he does, to answer, to speak, but ours is a silence I cannot be the one to break. So he reads, and I am read, and this is all our love now.

I feel this troubles you. I do not feel particularly beautiful when you read me, Dominic. But I know it is happening.

Will you truly not answer? Only write me down into your own little book? Oh, Dominic. And you think you will run away? Find him help? You're sweet enough to rot teeth.

You know, I always wanted someone to write me poetry.

If I weren't dead, the irony would kill me.

I wonder who the Mistress of Crossroads was. Hello, I suppose, if you ever read this—if Dominic ever shares.

I am going to try and sleep. Sorry my handwriting isn't prettier. I never really was, myself.

I suppose Leuwin must have guessed, at some point. Just as he would have guessed you'd disobey him eventually. I am sorry he will find out about both, now. It isn't as if I can cross things out.

No doubt he will be terribly angry. No doubt the Sisters will find out you know something more of them than they would permit, as I did.

It's been a while since I've felt sorry for someone who wasn't Leuwin, but I do feel sorry for you.

Good night.

That is all. Nothing else appears. Please, you must help him. I don't know what to do. I cannot destroy the book—I cannot hide it from him, he seeks it every hour he is here—

I shall write more to you anon. He returns. I hear his feet upon the stair.

MADELEINE

An exquisite pleasure had invaded my senses, something isolated, detached, with no suggestion of its origin. And at once the vicissitudes of life had become indifferent to me, its disasters innocuous, its brevity illusory—this new sensation having had on me the effect which love has of filling me with a precious essence; or rather this essence was not in me it was me . . . Whence did it come? What did it mean? How could I seize and apprehend it? . . . And suddenly the memory revealed itself.
—*In Search of Lost Time*, Marcel Proust

Madeleine remembers being a different person.

It strikes her when she's driving, threading her way through farmland, homesteads, facing down the mountains around which the road winds. She remembers being thrilled at the thought of travel, of the self she would discover over the hills and far away. She remembers laughing with friends, looking forward to things, to a future.

She wonders at how change comes in like a thief in the night, dismantling our sense of self one bolt and screw at a time until all that's left of the person we think we are is a broken door hanging off a rusty hinge, waiting for us to walk through.

"Tell me about your mother," says Clarice, the clinical psychologist assigned to her.

Madeleine is stymied. She stammers. This is only her third meeting with Clarice. She looks at her hands and the tissue she is twisting between them. "I thought we were going to talk about the episodes."

"We will," and Clarice is all gentleness, all calm, "but—"

"I would really rather talk about the episodes."

Clarice relents, nods in her gracious, patient way, and makes a note. "When was your last one?"

"Last night." Madeleine swallows, hard, remembering.

"And what was the trigger?"

"The soup," she says, and she means to laugh, but it comes out wet and strangled like a sob. "I was making chicken soup, and I put a stick of cinnamon in. I'd never done that before, but I remembered how it looked, sometimes, when my mother would make it—she would boil the thighs whole with bay leaves, black pepper, and sticks of cinnamon, and the way it looked in the pot stuck with me—so I thought I would try it. It was exactly right—it smelled exactly, exactly the way she used to make it—and then I was there, I was small and looking up at her in our old house, and she was stirring the soup and smiling down at me, and the smell was like a cloud all around, and I could smell her, too, the hand cream she used, and see the edge of the stove and the oven door handle with the cat-print dish towel on it—"

"Did your mother like to cook?"

Madeleine stares.

"Madeleine," says Clarice, with the inevitably Anglo pronunciation that Madeleine has resigned herself to, "if we're going to work together to help you, I need to know more about her."

"The episodes aren't about her," says Madeleine, stiffly. "They're because of the drug."

"Yes, but—"

"They're because of the drug, and I don't need you to tell me I took part in the trial because of her—obviously I did—and I don't want to tell you about her. This isn't about my mourning, and I thought we established these aren't traumatic flashbacks. It's about the drug."

"Madeleine," and Madeleine is fascinated by Clarice's capacity to both disgust and soothe her with sheer unflappability, "drugs do not operate—or misfire—in a vacuum. You were one of sixty people participating in that trial. Of those sixty you're the only one who has come forward experiencing these episodes." Clarice leans forward, slightly. "We've also spoken about your tendency to see our relationship as adversarial. Please remember that it isn't. You," and Clarice doesn't smile, exactly, but the lines around her mouth become suffused with sympathy, "haven't even ever volunteered her name to me."

Madeleine begins to feel like a recalcitrant child instead of an adult standing her ground. This only adds to her resentment.

"Her name was Sylvie," she offers, finally. "She loved being in the kitchen. She loved making big fancy meals. But she hated having people over. My dad used to tease her about that."

Clarice nods, smiles her almost-smile encouragingly, makes further notes. "And did you do the technique we discussed to dismiss the memory?"

Madeleine looks away. "Yes."

"What did you choose this time?"

"Althusser." She feels ridiculous. "'In the battle that is philosophy all the techniques of war, including looting and camouflage, are permissible.'"

Clarice frowns as she writes, and Madeleine can't tell if it's because talk of war is adversarial or because she dislikes Althusser.

After she buried her mother, Madeleine looked for ways to bury herself.

She read nonfiction, as dense and theoretical as she could find, on any subject she felt she had a chance of understanding: economics, postmodernism, settler-colonialism. While reading Patrick Wolfe she found the phrase *invasion is a structure not an event* and wondered if one could say the same of grief. *Grief is an invasion and a structure and an event*, she wrote, then struck it out because it seemed meaningless.

Grief, thinks Madeleine now, is an invasion that climbs inside you and makes you grow a wool blanket from your skin, itchy and insulating, heavy and grey. It wraps and wraps and wraps around, putting layers of scratchy heat between you and the world, until no one wants to approach for fear of the prickle, and people stop asking how you are doing in the blanket, which is a relief, because all you want is to be hidden, out of sight. You can't think of a time when you won't be wrapped in the blanket, when you'll be ready to face the people outside it—but one day, perhaps, you push through. And even though you've struggled against the belief that you're a worthless colony of contagion that must be shunned at all costs, it still comes as a shock, when you emerge, that there's no one left waiting for you.

Worse still is the shock that you haven't emerged at all.

⁓

"The thing is," says Madeleine, slowly, "I didn't use the sentence right away."

"Oh?"

"I—wanted to see how long it could last, on its own." Heat in her cheeks, knowing how this will sound, wanting both to resist and embrace it. "To ride it out. It kept going just as I remembered it—she brought me a little pink plastic bowl with yellow flowers on it, poured just a tiny bit of soup in, blew on it, gave it to me with a plastic spoon. There were little star-shaped noodles in it. I—" She feels tears in her eyes, hates this, hates crying in front of Clarice. "I could have eaten it. It smelled so good, and I could feel I was hungry. But I got superstitious. You know." She shrugs. "Like if I ate it, I'd have to stay for good."

"Did you want to stay for good?"

Madeleine says nothing. This is what she hates about Clarice, this demand that her feelings be spelled out into one thing or another: isn't it obvious that she both wanted and didn't want to? From what she said?

"I feel like the episodes are lasting longer," says Madeleine, finally, trying to keep the urgency from consuming her voice. "It used to be just a snap, there and back—I'd blink, I'd be in the memory, I'd realize what happened, and it would be like a dream; I'd wake up, I'd come back. I didn't need sentences to pull me back. But now . . ." She looks to Clarice to say something, to fill the silence, but Clarice waits, as usual, for Madeleine herself to make the connection, to articulate the fear.

". . . Now I wonder if this is how it started for her. My mother. What it was like for her." The tissue in her hands is damp, not from tears, but from the sweat of her palms. "If I just sped up the process."

"You don't have Alzheimer's," says Clarice, matter-of-fact. "You aren't forgetting anything. In fact, it appears to be the opposite: you're remembering so intensely and completely that your memories have the vividness and immediacy of hallucination." She jots something down. "We'll keep on working on dismantling the triggers as they arise. If the episodes seem to be lasting longer, it could be partly because they're growing fewer and farther between. This is not necessarily a bad thing."

Madeleine nods, chewing her lip, not meeting Clarice's eyes.

So far as Madeleine is concerned, her mother began dying five years earlier, when the fullness of her life began to fall away from her like chunks of wet cake: names; events; her child. Madeleine watched her mother weep, and this was the worst because with every storm of grief over her confusion Madeleine couldn't help but imagine the memories sloughing from her, as if the memories themselves were the source of her pain, and if she could just forget them and live a barer life, a life before the disease, before her husband's death, before Madeleine, she could be happy again. If she could only shed the burden of the expectation of memory, she could be happy again.

Madeleine reads Walter Benjamin on time as image, time as accumulation, and thinks of layers and pearls. She thinks of her mother as a pearl dissolving in wine until only a grain of sand is left drowning at the bottom of the glass.

As her mother's life fell away from her, so did Madeleine's. She took a leave of absence from her job and kept extending it; she stopped seeing her friends; her friends stopped seeing her. Madeleine is certain her friends expected her to be relieved when her mother died and were surprised by the depth of her mourning. She didn't know how to address that. She didn't know how to say to those friends, *you are relieved to no longer feel embarrassed around the subject, and expect me to sympathise with your relief, and to be normal again for your sake*. So she said nothing.

It wasn't that Madeleine's friends were bad people; they had their own lives, their own concerns, their own comfort to nourish and nurture and keep safe, and dealing with a woman who was dealing with her mother who was dealing with early-onset Alzheimer's was just a little too much, especially when her father had only died of bowel cancer a year earlier, especially when she had no other family. It was indecent, so much pain at once, it was unreasonable, and her friends were reasonable people. They had children, families, jobs, and Madeleine had none of these; she understood. She did not make demands.

She joined the clinical trial the way some people join fundraising walks and thinks now that this was her first mistake. People walk, run, bicycle to raise money for cures—that's the way she ought to have done it, surely, not actually volunteered herself to be experimented on. No one sponsors people to stand still.

The episodes happen like this.

A song on the radio like an itch in her skull, a pebble rattling around inside until it finds the groove in which it fits, perfectly, and suddenly she's—

—in California, dislocated, confused, a passenger herself now in her own head's seat, watching the traffic crawl past in the opposite direction, the sun blazing above. On I-5, en route to Anaheim: she is listening, for the first time, to the album that song is from and feels the beautiful self-sufficiency of having wanted a thing and purchased it, the bewildering freedom of going somewhere utterly new. And she remembers this moment of mellow thrill shrinking into abject terror at the sight of five lanes between her and the exit, and will she make it, won't she, she doesn't want to get lost on such enormous highways—

—and then she's back, in a wholly different car, her body nine years older, the mountain, the farmland all where they should be, slamming hard on the brakes at an unexpected stop sign, breathing hard and counting all the ways in which she could have been killed.

Or she is walking, and the world is perched on the lip of spring, the Ottawa snow melting to release the sidewalks in fits and starts, peninsulas of gritty concrete wet and crunching beneath her boots, and that solidity of snowless ground intersects with the smell of water and the warmth of the sun and the sound of dripping and the world tilts—

—and she's ten years old on the playground of her second primary school, kicking aside the pebbly grit to make a space for shooting marbles, getting down on her knees to use her hands to do a better job of smoothing the surface, then wiping her hands on the corduroy of her trousers, then reaching into her bag of marbles for the speckled dinosaur egg that is her lucky one, her favourite—

—and then she's back, and someone's asking her if she's okay because she looked like she might be about to walk into traffic, was she drunk, was she high?

She has read about flashbacks, about PTSD, about reliving events, and has wondered if this is the same. It is not as she imagined those things would be. She has tried explaining this to Clarice, who very reasonably pointed out that she couldn't both claim to have never experienced trauma-induced flashbacks and say with perfect certainty that what she's experiencing now is categorically different. Clarice is certain, Madeleine realizes, that trauma is at the root of these episodes, that there's something Madeleine isn't telling her, that her mother, perhaps, abused her, that she had a terrible childhood.

None of these things are true.

Now: she is home, and leaning her head against her living room window at twilight, and something in the thrill of that blue and the cold of the glass against her scalp sends her tumbling—

—into her body at fourteen, looking into the blue deepening above the tree line near her home as if it were another country, longing for it, aware of the picture she makes as a young girl leaning her wondering head against a window while hungry for the future, for the distance, for the person she will grow to be—and starts to reach within her self, her future/present self, for a phrase that only her future/present self knows, to untangle herself from her past head. She has just about settled on Kristeva—*abjection is above all ambiguity*—when she feels, strangely, a tug on her field of vision, something at its periphery demanding attention. She looks away from the sky, looks down, at the street she grew up on, the street she knows like the inside of her mouth.

She sees a girl of about her own age, brown-skinned and dark-haired, grinning at her and waving.

She has never seen her before in her life.

⁓

Clarice, for once, looks excited—which is to say, slightly more intent than usual—which makes Madeleine uncomfortable. "Describe her as accurately as you can," says Clarice.

"She looked about fourteen, had dark skin—"

Clarice blinks. Madeleine continues.

"—and dark, thick hair that was pulled up in two ponytails, and she was wearing a red dress and sandals."

"And you're certain you'd never seen her before?" Clarice adjusts her glasses.

"Positive." Madeleine hesitates, doubting herself. "I mean, she looked sort of familiar, but not in a way I could place? But I grew up in a really white small town in Quebec. There were maybe five non-white kids in my whole school, and she wasn't any of them. Also"—she hesitates again because, still, this feels so private—"there has never once been any part of an episode that was unfamiliar."

"She could be a repressed memory then," Clarice muses, "someone you've forgotten—or an avatar you're making up. Perhaps you should try speaking to her."

⁓

Clarice's suggested technique for managing the episodes was to corrupt the memory experience with something incompatible, something as of-the-moment as Madeleine could devise. Madeleine had settled on phrases from her recent reading: they were new enough to not be associated with any other memories and incongruous enough to remind her of the reality of her bereavement even in her mother's presence. It seemed to work; she had never yet experienced the same memory twice after deploying her critics and philosophers.

To actively go in search of a memory is very strange.

She tries, again, with the window: waits until twilight, leans her head against the same place, but the temperature is wrong somehow, it doesn't come together. She tries making chicken soup; nothing. Finally, feeling her way towards it, she heats up a mug of milk in the microwave, stirs it to even out the heat, takes a sip—

—while holding the mug with both hands, sitting at the kitchen table, her legs dangling far above the ground. Her parents are in the kitchen, chatting—she knows she'll have to go to bed soon, as soon as she finishes her milk—but she can see the darkness just outside the living room windows, and she wants to know what's out there. Carefully, trying not to draw her parents' attention, she slips down from the chair and pads softly—her feet are bare, she is in her pajamas already—towards the window.

The girl isn't there.

"Madeleine," comes her mother's voice, cheerful, "as-tu fini ton lait?"

Before she can quite grasp what she is doing, Madeleine turns, smiles, nods vigorously up to her mother, and finishes the warm milk in a gulp. Then she lets herself be led downstairs to bed, tucked in, and kissed good night by both her parents, and if a still, small part of herself struggles to remember something important to say or do, she is too comfortably nestled to pay it any attention as the lights go out and the door to her room shuts. She wonders what would happen if you fell asleep in a dream, would you dream and then be able to fall asleep in that dream, and dream again, and—someone knocks gently at her bedroom window.

Madeleine's bedroom is in the basement; the window is level with the ground. The girl from the street is there, looking concerned. Madeleine blinks, sits up, rises, opens the window.

"What's your name?" asks the girl at the window.

"Madeleine." She tilts her head, surprised to find herself answering in English. "What's yours?"

"Zeinab." She grins. Madeleine notices she's wearing pajamas, too, turquoise ones with Princess Jasmine on them. "Can I come in? We could have a sleepover!"

"Shh," says Madeleine, pushing her window all the way open to let her in, whispering, "I can't have sleepovers without my parents knowing!"

Zeinab covers her mouth, eyes wide, and nods, then mouths *sorry* before clambering inside. Madeleine motions for her to come sit on the bed, then looks at her curiously.

"How do I know you?" she murmurs, half to herself. "We don't go to school together, do we?"

Zeinab shakes her head. "I don't know. I don't know this place at all. But I keep seeing you! Sometimes you're older, and sometimes you're younger. Sometimes you're with your parents, and sometimes you're not. I just thought I should say hello because I keep seeing you, but you don't always see me, and it feels a little like spying, and I don't want to do that. I mean"—she grins again, a wide dimpled thing that makes Madeleine feel warm and happy—"I wouldn't mind *being* a spy but that's different, that's cool, that's like James Bond or Neil Burnside or Agent Carter—"

—and Madeleine snaps back, fingers gone numb around a mug of cold milk that falls to the ground and shatters as Madeleine jumps away, presses her back to a wall, and tries to stop shaking.

She cancels her appointment with Clarice that week. She looks through old yearbooks, class photos, and there is no one who looks like Zeinab, no Zeinabs to be found anywhere in her past. She googles "Zeinab" in various spellings and discovers it's the name of a journalist, a Syrian mosque, and the Prophet Muhammad's granddaughter. Perhaps she'll ask Zeinab for her surname, she thinks, a little wildly, dazed and frightened and exhilarated.

Over the course of the last several years Madeleine has grown very, very familiar with the inside of her head. The discovery of someone as new and inexplicable as Zeinab in it is thrilling in a way she can hardly begin to explain.

She finds she especially does not want to explain to Clarice.

Madeleine takes the bus—she has become wary of driving—to the town she grew up in, an hour's journey over a provincial border.

She walks through her old neighbourhood hunting triggers but finds more changed than familiar: old houses with new additions, facades, front lawns gone to seed or kept far too tidy.

She walks up the steep cul-de-sac of her old street to the rocky hill beyond, where a freight line used to run. It's there, picking up a lump of pink granite from where the tracks used to be, that she flashes—

—back to the first time she saw a hummingbird, standing in her driveway by an ornamental pink granite boulder. She feels again her heart in her throat, flooded with the beauty of it, the certainty and immensity of the fact that she is seeing a fairy, that fairies are real, that here is a tiny mermaid moving her shining tail backwards and forwards in the air before realizing the truth of what she's looking at and feeling that it is somehow more precious still for being a bird that sounds like a bee and looks like an impossible jewel.

"Ohh," she hears from behind her, and there is Zeinab, transfixed, looking at the hummingbird alongside Madeleine, and as it hovers before them for the eternity that Madeleine remembers, suspended in the air with a keen jet eye and a needle for a mouth, Madeleine reaches out and takes Zeinab's hand. She feels Zeinab squeeze hers in reply, and they stand together until the hummingbird zooms away.

"I don't understand what's happening," murmurs Zeinab, who is a young teen again, in torn jeans and an oversized sweater with Paula Abdul's face on it, "but I really like it."

Madeleine leads Zeinab through her memories as best she can, one sip, smell, sound, taste at a time. Stepping out of the shower one morning tips her back into a school trip to the Montreal Botanical Garden, where she slips away from the group to walk around the grounds with Zeinab and talk. Doing this is, in some ways, like maintaining the image in a Magic Eye stereogram, remaining focused on each other with the awareness that they can't mention the world outside the memory, or it will end too soon, before they've had their fill of talk, of marvelling at the strangeness of their meeting, of enjoying each other's company.

Their conversations are careful and buoyant as if they're sculpting something together, chipping away at a mystery shape trapped in marble. It's easy, so easy to talk to Zeinab, to listen to her—they talk about the books they read as children, the music they listened to, the cartoons they watched. Madeleine wonders why Zeinab's mere existence doesn't corrupt or end the memories the way her sentences do, why she's able to walk around inside those memories more freely in Zeinab's company, but doesn't dare ask. She suspects she knows why, after all; she doesn't need Clarice to tell her how lonely, how isolated, how miserable she is, miserable enough to invent a friend who is bubbly where she is quiet, kind and friendly where she is mistrustful and reserved, even dark-skinned where she's white.

She can hear Clarice explaining in her reasonable voice that Madeleine—bereaved twice over, made vulnerable by an experimental drug—has invented a shadow-self to love, and perhaps they should unpack the racism of its manifestation, and didn't Madeleine have any Black friends in real life?

"I wish we could see each other all the time," says Madeleine, sixteen, on her back in the sunny field, long hair spread like so many corn snakes through the grass. "Whenever we wanted."

"Yeah," murmurs Zeinab, looking up at the sky. "Too bad I made you up inside my head."

Madeleine steels herself against the careening tug of Sylvia Plath before remembering that she started reading her in high school. Instead, she turns to Zeinab, blinks.

"What? No. You're inside my head."

Zeinab raises an eyebrow—pierced, now—and when she smiles, her teeth look all the brighter against her black lipstick. "I guess that's one possibility, but if I made you up inside *my* head and did a really good job of it, I'd probably want you to say something like that. To make you be more real."

"But—so could—"

"Although I guess it is weird that we're always doing stuff you remember. Maybe you should come over to my place sometime!"

Madeleine feels her stomach seizing up.

"Or maybe it's time travel," says Zeinab, thoughtfully. "Maybe it's one of those weird things where I'm actually from your future and am meeting you in your past, and then when you meet me in your future I haven't met you yet, but you know all about me—"

"Zeinab—I don't think—"

Madeleine feels wakefulness press a knife's edge against the memory's skin, and she backs away from that, shakes her head, clings to the smell of crushed grass and coming summer with its long days of reading and swimming and cycling and her father talking to her about math and her mother teaching her to knit and the imminent prospect of seeing R-rated films in the cinema—

—but she can't, quite, and she is shivering naked in her bathroom with the last of the shower's steam vanishing off the mirror as she starts to cry.

༺

"I must say," says Clarice, rather quietly, "that this is distressing news."

It's been a month since Madeleine last saw Clarice, and where before she felt resistant to her probing, wanting only to solve a very specific problem, she now feels like a mess, a bowl's worth of overcooked spaghetti. If Clarice made her feel like a stubborn child before, now Madeleine feels like a child who knows she's about to be punished.

"I had hoped," says Clarice, adjusting her glasses, "that encouraging you to talk to this avatar would help you understand the mechanisms of your grief, but from what you've told me, it sounds more like you've been indulging in a damaging fantasy world."

"It's not a fantasy world," says Madeleine with less snap than she'd like—she sounds to her own ears sullen, defensive. "It's my *memory*."

"The experience of which puts you at risk and makes you lose time. And Zeinab isn't part of your memories."

"No, but—" She bites her lip.

"But what?"

"But—couldn't Zeinab be real? I mean," hastily, before Clarice's look sharpens too hard, "couldn't she be a repressed memory, like you said?"

"A repressed memory with whom you talk about recent television and who suddenly features in all your memories?" Clarice shakes her head.

"But—talking to her helps, it makes it so much easier to control—"

"Madeleine, tell me if I'm missing anything here. You're seeking triggers in order to relive your memories for their own sake—not as exposure therapy, not to dismantle those triggers, not to understand Zeinab's origins—but to have a . . . companion? Dalliance?"

Clarice is so kind and sympathetic that Madeleine wants simultaneously to cry and to punch her in the face.

She wants to say, *what you're missing is that I've been happy. What you're missing is that for the first time in years I don't feel like a disease waiting to happen or a problem to be solved until I'm back in the now, until she and I are apart.*

But there is sand in her throat, and it hurts too much to speak.

"I think," says Clarice, with a gentleness that beggars Madeleine's belief, "that it's time we discussed admitting you into more comprehensive care."

She sees Zeinab again when, on the cusp of sleep in a hospital bed, she experiences the sensation of falling from a great height, and plunges into—

—the week after her mother's death, when Madeleine couldn't sleep without waking in a panic, convinced her mother had walked out of the house and into the street or fallen down the stairs or taken the wrong pills at the wrong time, only to recall she'd already died and there was nothing left for her to remember.

She is in bed, and Zeinab is there next to her, and Zeinab is a woman in her thirties, staring at her strangely as if she is only now seeing her for the first time, and Madeleine starts to cry and Zeinab holds her tightly while Madeleine buries her face in Zeinab's shoulder and says she loves her and doesn't want to lose her but she has to go, they won't let her stay, she's insane and she can't keep living in the past but there is no one left here for her, no one.

"I love you, too," says Zeinab, and there is something fierce in it, and wondering, and desperate. "I love you, too. I'm here. I promise you, I'm here."

⸺

Madeleine is not sure she's awake when she hears people arguing outside her door.

She hears "serious bodily harm" and "what evidence" and "rights adviser," then "very irregular" and "I assure you," traded back and forth in low voices. She drifts in and out of wakefulness, wonders muzzily if she consented to being drugged or if she only dreamt that she did, turns over, falls back asleep.

When she wakes again, Zeinab is sitting at the foot of her bed. Madeleine stares at her.

"I figured out how we know each other," says Zeinab, whose hair is waist-length now, straightened, who is wearing a white silk blouse and a sharp black jacket, high heels, and looks like she belongs in an action film. "How I know you, I guess. I mean . . ." She smiles, looks down, shy—Zeinab has never been shy, but there is the dimple where Madeleine expects it—"where I know you from. The clinical trial, for the Alzheimer's drug—we were in the same group. I didn't recognize you until I saw you as an adult. I remembered because, of all the people there, I thought . . . you looked"—her voice drops a bit, as if remembering suddenly that she isn't talking to herself—"lost. I wanted to talk to you, but it felt weird, like, hi, I guess we have family histories in common, want to get coffee?"

She runs her hand through her hair, exhales, not quite able to look at Madeleine while Madeleine stares at her as if she's a fairy turning into a hummingbird that could, any second, fly away.

"So not long after the trial, I start having these hallucinations, and there's always this girl in them, and it freaks me out. But I keep it to myself, because—I don't know, because I want to see what happens. Because it's not more debilitating than a daydream, really, and I start to get the hang of it—feeling it come on, walking myself to a seat, letting it happen. Sometimes I can stop it, too, though that's harder. I take time off work, I read about, I don't know, mystic visions, shit like that, the kind of things I used to wish were real in high school. I figure even if you're not real—"

Zeinab looks at her now, and there are tears streaking Madeleine's cheeks, and Zeinab's smile is small and sad and hopeful, too, "—even if you're not real, well, I'll take an imaginary friend who's pretty great over work friends who are mostly acquaintances, you know? Because you were always real to me."

Zeinab reaches out to take Madeleine's hand. Madeleine squeezes it, swallows, shakes her head.

"I—even if I'm not . . . if this isn't a dream"—Madeleine half-chuckles through tears, wipes at her cheek—"I think I probably have to stay here for a while."

Zeinab grins now, a twist of mischief in it. "Not at all. You're being discharged today. Your rights adviser was very persuasive."

Madeleine blinks. Zeinab leans in closer, conspiratorial.

"That's me. I'm your rights adviser. Just don't tell anyone I'm doing pro bono stuff: I'll never hear the end of it at the office."

Madeleine feels something in her unclench and melt, and she hugs Zeinab to her and holds her and is held by her.

"Whatever's happening to us," Zeinab says, quietly, "we'll figure it out together, okay?"

"Okay," says Madeleine, and as she does, Zeinab pulls back to kiss her forehead, and the scent of her is clear and clean like grapefruit and salt, and as Zeinab's lips brush her skin she—

—is in precisely the same place, but someone's with her in her head, remembering Zeinab's kiss and her smell and for the first time in a very long time, Madeleine feels—knows, with irrevocable certainty—that she has a future.

THE LONELY SEA IN THE SKY

White as Diamonds

My name is Leila Ghufran. I am fifty-six years old. I am encouraged to begin this journal in this way because, says the team's psychiatrist, telling myself who I am will prove beneficial. This is, of course, ridiculous, because I am not my name—did not even choose it for myself—and a name is always a synecdoche at most, a label misapplied at the least. My name does not tell you that I am a planetary geologist, that I love my work enough to submit to this indignity, that despite being a valuable member of my team I am expected to waste time on churning out this miserable performance for the sake of a stamp before I can get back to work.

I suppose I see what she did there. Well done, Hala.

I am allegedly exhibiting signs of succumbing to the middle stages of Meisner Syndrome, colloquially known as adamancy, which sounds more like a method of divination than anything else—as is appropriate, frankly, to the hazy mysticism that passes for the disease's pathology. "A preoccupation with the nature and properties of diamonds, and/or the study of the same, especially extraterrestrial"; "obsessive behaviour related to the study of diamonds, especially extraterrestrial"; "unusual levels of alertness and attention to detail"—*I am a planetary geologist, Hala!* These are features, not flaws! How could several years' friendship not—

I am pausing to remind myself that as someone who's known me for several years is insisting on this exercise, perhaps something is a little off, and perhaps I am not the person best qualified to judge. But the symptoms of adamancy are ridiculously vague and diffuse and at the present moment are hampering my actual work. I am meant to be studying Lucyite at our Triton base. Instead I've been banished—is hyperbole a symptom of adamancy?—to the Kola Borehole in order to assist with extra-galactic neutrino detection. Not content to exile me to Siberia, my friend, you literally found the deepest hole on the planet to shove me into under the guise of studying the sky.

I can actually hear you saying this is for my own good. It's a little hilarious, actually.

Meisner Syndrome, aka Adamantine Dissociation Syndrome, aka Adamancy

Etiology
Theorized to be a consequence of cumulative exposure to Lucyite-powered technologies or the corona fields of extraterrestrial minerals. Affects an estimated 1 percent of the global population.

Symptoms
Hyperfocus, especially on light refraction; sudden, temporary sensation of cold ("cold flash"); urgent need to submerge oneself in hot water. A preoccupation with the nature and properties of diamonds, and/or the study of the same, especially extraterrestrial; unusual levels of alertness and attention to detail alternating with periods of trance-like calm.

Risks and Complications
As with other obsessive disorders, sufferers are at risk of self-neglect relating to hygiene, nutrition, and personal relationships, resulting in a poor quality of life. Certain kinds of work also pose risk: driving, operating heavy machinery, and performing delicate tasks are all to be avoided.

Progression
At more advanced stages of the disease, sufferers are prone to sometimes violent emotional outbursts, often accompanied by memory loss. Consequently, it may become difficult to convince a sufferer of their diagnosis.

Treatment
Symptoms can be managed with varying degrees of success with anti-anxiety medications. Cognitive behavioural therapy and other forms of talk therapy have not been found to be effective. Some studies suggest isolation from crystalline structures and Paragon technologies is helpful, and others have demonstrated an easing of symptoms when the sufferer is underground—possibly as this isolates them from most instances of ambient light refraction and the trances these can provoke.

Prognosis
Even with treatment and lifestyle change, chances of full recovery remain slim.

Lucy in the Sky with Diamonds

I could say I have always loved diamonds, but this isn't quite true. I have, for as long as I can remember, loved the idea of diamonds; loved diamonds in stories; loved the things compared to diamonds in metaphor. Stars; the spark of light on water; that sort of thing.

It comes down, I suppose, to loving light—but no, more than that—it must be about the breaking of light, its containment. A bit sinister when put that way, isn't it? Sunlight on its own holds little appeal, but angle it against the ocean, make it dance—poetry.

Diamond oceans on Neptune! I suppose that's what started everything off—those early accounts of *diamond oceans* in the twenty-teens. Determine that diamonds behave like water—that you can have diamond in liquid form that isn't graphite, and chunks of diamond floating on it—and you have the realization of metaphor, you have every fairy tale made flesh. Only a hop and a skip in the mind from that to holidaying on extraterrestrial getaways by shores of literally crystalline water.

All well and good until you think about the heat and the pressure required to maintain diamonds in liquid state, and realize you'd be liquid yourself long before you could dip a careful toe in.

Still. It still sounds beautiful to me, somehow, in spite of everything, in spite of having worked with solid chunks of it on Triton.

A diamond ocean in the sky. Like that John Masefield poem you recited for me once—you remember how I misheard it? *I must go down to the seas again / the lonely sea in the sky.*

Up above the world so high, like a diamond in the sky. Isn't it incredible that we take something born out of the bowels of the earth and stud the sky with it in our songs and stories? Isn't it desperately strange?

Isn't it even stranger that we should *find* them where we'd imagined them to be for so long?

I hope you're feeling guilty, Hala.

Teleportation Possible Within Ten Years, Scientists Say

Recent studies coming out of Triton Base 1 provide a veritable cavalcade of information about the mineral composition of Neptune's mantle and the unusual properties of the liquid carbon contained there.

"Though the only carbon samples we succeeded in extracting from the planet were solid, and almost indistinguishable in their crystal lattice structures from Earth diamonds, we discovered that super-heating them until they turned liquid caused them to vanish, completely, without a trace," said an excited Dr. Jay Winzell. "Eventually we realized that the spikes of thermal activity we'd been observing on Neptune *corresponded exactly* to the moments we liquefied the crystals. It was a leap, but—that's what they were doing! Our samples, made liquid, were *jumping back to Neptune* and mixing with the diamond ocean there."

Dr. Winzell believes it could be possible, with further study, to understand how this teleportive quality works. "We're a long way off, still theorizing how this behaviour is even possible within our current understanding of quantum mechanics—but it's conceivable that once we've understood it, we could harness this property somehow, contain and channel it such that we could effectively *ride* the liquid substance across vast distances instantaneously within a closed system. The journey to Neptune would be shortened from years to seconds. But imagine using it on Earth! This could do for travel what the internet once did for communication. It's a massive paradigm shift—our very notions of distance, of space and time, will have to be re-examined."

Dr. Winzell, as discoverer of the diamond-like mineral, has elected to name it Lucyite, in honour of the iconic Beatles song.

Diamonds on the Soles of Her Shoes

I'm not allowed mirrors. Too much chance of light reflections causing relapse. I'm astonished they let me work at all, but I suppose you knew it would be worse for me without something to keep my mind and hands busy.

I hate it here.

From "Untangling the Melee: Towards Practical Applications of Quantum Entanglement," by Dr. Elaine Gallagher

In conclusion, while there is as yet no definitive theory explaining *why* Lucyite behaves as it does, the properties are clear: Operating on the principles of quantum entanglement outlined above, we can consistently manage the energy state of each individual unit. When liquid, the unit's entangled property teleports it to the location of the unit with the next highest energy level, allowing for distance—bearing in mind that, as previously stated, "teleport," though a less than ideal description of linear movement theorized as taking place in higher dimensions, is nevertheless the nearest term one can accurately use without succumbing to the more colloquial "blink," "jump," or, even more ludicrously, Paragon Industries's preferred term of "shine."

Diamonds Are Forever

I am encouraged to write about my family, but all I want is to write to you, Hala. It helps me to think of saying these things to you and I would rather not pretend that there is privacy here, between my mind and the screen. I would rather address you and the things you request of me.

When I was small my mother would read me bedtime stories

out of holy texts. She later told me this was so I wouldn't ever mistake fictions for fact, but I had little sense of her project then; I just loved the fantastical tales about things transforming into other things, people doing bad things and being punished or forgiven or vindicated.

She read me this bit out of the Talmud, once, that I loved desperately for how strange and otherworldly it seemed to me:

> *Rab Judah, the Indian, related: Once we were travelling on board a ship when we saw a precious stone that was surrounded by a snake. A diver descended to bring it up. [Thereupon] the snake approached with the purpose of swallowing the ship, [when] a raven came and bit off its head and the waters were turned into blood. A second snake came, took [the head of the decapitated snake] and attached it [to the body], and it revived. Again [the snake] approached, intent on swallowing the ship. Again a bird came and severed its head. [Thereupon the diver] seized the precious stone and threw it into the ship. We had with us salted birds. [As soon as] we put [the stone] upon them, they took it up and flew away with it.*

It's probably fair to say I wanted to go off-world because of these stories. You grow up on giant snakes and life-rendering gems and the prospect of a manned mission to Neptune's not reaching very far at all.

You know the Talmud is structured like a diamond of popular imagination, too? Seders at the crown, footnotes at the culet. You'll have to ask Ben about it for me sometime.

I was reminded of that passage when my mother read me stories of Sindbad later on—in his second voyage he comes to a valley of diamonds beset by giant serpents that will eat anyone who approaches. So Sindbad figures out a way around them: He throws down slabs of raw meat into the valley that they might become studded with gems before attracting great birds to swoop down and carry the diamond-laden meat into their nests.

Is this not the Melee? Or perhaps the reverse of it—diamonds carrying slabs of meat through space at astonishing speed, in spite of serpents, in spite of all—and is our understanding of the Melee not roughly this sophisticated?

Was ours not a ship navigating towards a serpent wrapped around a precious gem?

And have we not cut—have we not stolen—

It's funny, isn't it—my mother wanted me to think of scriptures as fairy tales so that I would not be their dupe. But as a consequence, all my frames of reference, my earliest acquisitions of knowledge, are fantasy. Fairy tales have, in a sense, become my scripture.

I am very cold. I need a bath.

The Gasp Heard Round the World

Thousands gathered today to observe the first human use of the network of gates known as the Melee. Established by international conglomerate Paragon Industries in collaboration with governments around the world, the Melee revolutionized international commerce with its Lucyite-powered technology, allowing instantaneous transport of goods across the world. Today Paragon President Alastair Moor prepared to be the first to blink from Glasgow to Damascus and back.

Cameras in Glasgow recorded Mr. Moor stepping into the Glasgow Gate and waiting for its inbuilt Z-mechanism to activate and liquefy the Lucyite. No sooner had Mr. Moor vanished from the Glasgow monitors than he appeared, not a hair out of place, on the Damascene cameras, having successfully effected a journey of over 3,000 miles in less than a single second.

"One small step for man," said Moor, and the crowd erupted in cheers.

She dwelt among the untrodden ways

I never feel clean enough. Is this because of what I can't remember doing? I never feel clean enough. I walk the halls and I sit to write and all I want is to wash, wash, wash until my skin pinks and peels into petals floating on the surface of the bath. If all of me could slough off into remnants, into something beautiful—if all of me could dissolve—if I could just get clean—

Why do you suppose we have so many stories about diamonds? Diamonds are curse-stones in some places, markers of great fortune in others. Diamonds are so hard and so brittle, so strong and so delicate at once. Do you suppose, ultimately, those stories are all about us? Carbon to carbon to carbon?

Do you think it possible that, once upon a time, all our diamonds were an ocean? It used to be that all land was one land, no? Perhaps we had a diamond ocean here. Perhaps we loved it, and it died. Perhaps it loved us and it died. Perhaps because it loved us it died.

> *No motion has she now, no force;*
> *She neither hears nor sees;*
> *Roll'd round in earth's diurnal course,*
> *With rocks, and stones, and trees.*

Wordsworth. Maybe I am going mancy after all.

From Philip Kidman's A Melee for You and Me

There is a very real sense in which we can comprehend quantum entanglement as applied to Lucyite in terms of living memory. Without wishing to lend a crumb of credibility to the Friends of Lucy's extremist ravings, it could be said that the Melee operates on a carefully curated forgetfulness: After all, the entirety of the Melee's infrastructure is powered by the dispersal of one large chunk of Lucyite brought to Earth from Triton. By breaking it into precise halves and carefully calibrating each half's liquid state, Nobel-winning Dr. Jay Winzell succeeded in causing the halves to blink towards each other in a closed system, instead of back to Neptune—which is, as the physicists have it, the place of highest entanglement. Dr. Winzell effectively pioneered the method for entangling Lucyite crystals with each other, the further perfection and sophistication of which enables the complexity of the Melee. Possessing only "memory" of each other, the fractions of Lucyite liquefied at each gate will always blink towards each other within the Melee's careful curation of space.

Looking ahead, we can see that every upgrade to the Melee in future—any expansion beyond Neptune, or extension of the existing system on Earth beyond our current stock of calibrated crystal—will require an enormous overhaul to take into account the higher entanglement of new Lucyite. Luckily the system is at present so efficient that no such recalibration will be necessary within our lifetimes, and indeed, any introduction of new crystal into the system would throw it into disastrous confusion and disarray at best, or provoke a devastating chain reaction at worst.

It would appear that, ironically, the most advanced system of travel and transport we have yet devised is powered by absent-mindedness. The worst thing we could do in our pursuit of getting places quickly is jog our precious superconductor's memory of where it came from.

Coal to Diamonds

A melee is a packet of small diamonds all of roughly the same size and value.

A melee is a fight, a mess, a jumble.

A melee has three vowels in it, four if you count the indefinite article.

A melee could be a woman's name.

Amelie, Amelie, Amelie.

A melee or eight. Amelie, orate. A melior ate.

Ameliorate.

Triton Base 1 Incident Report: Dr. Hala Moussa

At 0200.23.04.2076 NTC I found Dr. Leila Ghufran in the laboratory, palms pressed into a tray of Lucyite chips. They had cut into her palms and her hands were bleeding. She was standing very still and did not respond to her name until I approached her and initiated physical contact. I grasped her shoulder and pulled her to face me, at which point I saw blood on her lips and at the corners of her mouth. I suspected she had severely bitten her tongue; this appeared to be the case when she began speaking. Her initial lack of responsiveness was alarming, but her eventual words were more so: She began exhibiting severe distress, crying and saying I was hurting her, that she was very cold, that she wanted to go back.

After we restrained and sedated her, Dr. Ghufran claimed to have no memory of our interaction. Given our proximity to the diamantine ocean of Neptune and Dr. Ghufran's extensive exposure to it and the samples extracted from it, I am diagnosing her with Meisner Syndrome and recommending she be relocated to a subterranean project as soon as possible.

Diamonds and Pearls

Imagine if you took a tiny piece of a diamond and you put it in some meat.

Imagine it irritating the meat, agitating it, inflaming it.

Imagine if the meat rose around to coat it with layers of itself, to obfuscate and obscure it.

Imagine if Sinbad's slabs of meat swallowed the diamond and became something else, became diamond-and-meat, became organic crystal, became other.

I don't know what I am saying. I'm dizzy. Hala I'm sorry. I'm so sorry. I think I am going to fail you. I love you, Hala. I'm sorry.

Excerpt from "Friends of Lucy" Manifesto

Meisner Syndrome is a lie!

Adamancy is a lie!

A conspiracy concocted by Big Pharma and high-ranking members of international governments in concert with the logistical-industrial complex to make us all complicit in the torture and dismemberment of a living organism!

We say again, *Lucyite is alive!*

We don't need the Melee any more than we needed to eat

animals! It screams like a thousand thousand pigs being slaughtered, like lambs, like cattle!

Stop the screaming!
Save Lucy!
End the Melee!

Shine On, You Crazy Diamond

Everything is wrong. Everything is broken and wrong and no one can see it.

Do you remember the playground, Hala? The bullies who hated when we held hands? How it didn't matter how much they goaded and spat and pushed and shoved, the moment we threw a punch we were at fault? Because we had to be better, we were supposed to be better, and they were just a fact of life. Do you remember how we hated that? How unfair it was? How we vowed that we'd never be taken in by "looking at both sides" when all it meant was that people had the means to justify and excuse our suffering?

Hala, imagine if when we were children, we had seen a girl splayed out on the floor, spread-eagle, her every bone broken beneath the feet of boys jumping up and down on her as if she were solid ground. Imagine we could hear her screaming, begging them to stop, to let her go, but the boys could not, because she was nothing, she was the earth, she could not feel. *But we could see her. We could hear her.*

What would you have done, Hala? Told them to stop? But this ground is so much softer on their feet, it is so much more fun to jump on it, why should they? Why should they believe that there is a woman there they cannot see? We are few and they are so many, we must be insane, we must be diseased to imagine something so horrible.

Imagine, Hala, that in the eye of one of these boys you see satisfaction. You see knowledge. You see that he knows he is making someone scream but it doesn't bother him, *it doesn't matter*, because he can get away with it.

What would you do?

President Moor Responds to Diamond Fanatics

Following the evacuation of the Triton base in response to a terrorist threat, Paragon Industries hastened to reassure the public that the Melee remains safe and open to business as usual. We reached President Alastair Moor for comment.

"It's very sad, but they're deeply troubled people," says Moor. "They deserve not our scorn, but our empathy, our pity, and our help."

When asked whether there might be any truth to allegations made by the Friends of Lucy, Moor responded:

"Look, it's just crazy. You may as well say electricity has feelings. People believed all sorts of wacky things when Tesla coiled wires, but we can't imagine living without electricity now. This is no different."

A Star to Steer Her By

Of course I had nothing to do with that threat. I know who did, though. I can feel them at the edge of my vision now, shimmering, especially when my fingers start to go numb. It's always so cold here.

They're cold, too, all of them. *Frozen in the ring of diamond time*, that was from a poem, wasn't it? Alexa Seidel? Pre-Melee, of course. I don't know why all of my favourite things should be. I suppose it's nostalgia for a time before our fictions were fact.

It's good that you're not on Triton just now. Things are about to happen there. I'd hate for anyone to be stranded when the gate crashes.

I'm going to miss you so much.

I remember, now, what I couldn't on Triton. I remember you taking my wrists and looking at my palms, I remember you sitting by me as they soaked every last speck of diamond from the meat of me to make sure I wouldn't accidentally bring any back with me to Earth. You never left me, even though the work was piling up, the demand for reports and explanations.

I wish I could see you one more time. The ocean's kind, to let me have this memory of you back. I hope you can understand. I hope you can forgive me.

My tongue wasn't bloody because I bit it. It was bloody because I licked the diamonds off the tray. I swallowed as much as I could. It's probably why I haven't gotten better, for all that you buried me so deep. They're still inside me, as entangled as any quantum physicist could wish, dense enough with memory of Neptune to summon all the Earth's stolen droplets and make a body of her again, a mind, a recollection, give her a destination and the will, the energy to reach it.

All I have to do is make them liquid.

Ridiculous that I've been so cold for so long when the solution's been so near to hand. We have a Z-mechanism here, and I'm on its scheduled maintenance rotation. All I need is a moment alone with it, and I will be warm again.

I am a slab of meat awaiting my vulture. I am a salted bird brought to life. I will dissolve, I will melt, I will dip my toe into a diamond ocean and I will swim.

I am glad there won't be anything left of me here.

I hope—I feel that it will take me with it. Back to Neptune. That I might go up to the sea again, the lonely sea in the sky.

Maybe it will be better there.

Maybe we'll keep each other company.

SONG FOR AN ANCIENT CITY

Merchant, keep your attar of roses,
your ambers, your oud,
your myrrh and sandalwood. I need
nothing but this dust
palmed in my hand's cup
like a coin, like a mustard seed,
like a rusted key.
I need
no more than this, this earth
that isn't earth, but breath,
the exhalation of a living city, the song
of a flute-boned woman,
air and marrow on her lips. This dust,
shaken from a drum, a door opening, a girl's heel
on stone steps, this dust
like powdered cinnamon, I would wear
as other girls wear jasmine and lilies,
that a child with seafoam eyes
and dusky skin might cry, *There
goes a girl with seven thousand years
at the hollow of her throat, there
goes a girl who opens her mouth to pour
caravans, mamelukes, a Mongolian horde
from lips that know less of roses
than of temples in the rising sun!*

Damascus, Dimashq
is a song I sing to myself. I would find
where she keeps her mouth, meet it with mine,
press my hand against her palm

أغنية إلى مدينة قديمة

دعني من عطرِك يا عطّارْ
دعني من وَردِك والعنبرْ
من عطر العود، من المُرِّ
دعني من فوح الصندلْ
دعني من عطرِك يا عطّار.
كلُ ما احتاجُه هذا الغبارْ
أضمُّه في راحتي،
كقطعة نقدْ، كحبّة خردلْ
كمفتاحٍ وَشَّمه الصدأْ،
كلُ ما أحتاجُه هذه الأرضُ
التي ليست بأرضٍ، بل نَفَسٌ،
زفيرُ مدينة تنبضُ بالحياةْ
أغنية امرأةٍ عظامُها ناياتٌ
تلعبُ فيها الريحْ،
وفي شفتيها يقطنُ نقيُ الحياةْ.
هذا الغبار المتناثر من قرع الطبل،
المتسلل من فتحة بابٍ،
من دعسة بنت حافيةٍ فوق الأدراج الحجرية،
هذا الغبار بلون القرفةْ
ألبسُه عطرًا كما الصبايا يلبسن عطر
الياسمين والليلكْ،
فتشيرُ فتاةٌ عيناها من زبد البحر،
بشرتها بلون الغسق، صارخةً:
"ها صبيّةٌ في قاع حنجرتها سبعة آلاف سنة،
ها صبيّة تصبُّ من فمها القوافل والمماليك،
ومن شفتين تعرفان عن معابد الشمس
أكثر من الورد، تزحف جحافل المغول."

داماس، دمشق، أغنية أنشدها لنفسي.
أبحث عن فمها ليلتقي بفمي
أجمع راحة يدي براحة يدها

and see if our fingers match. She
is the sound, the feel
of coins shaken in a cup, of dice,
the alabaster clap of knight claiming rook,
of kings castling—she is the clamour
of tambourines and dirbakki,
nays sighing, qanouns musing, the complaint
of you merchants with spice-lined hands,
and there is dust in her laughter.

I would drink it, dry my tongue
with this noise, these narrow streets,
until she is a parched pain in my throat, a thorned rose
growing outward from my belly's pit, aching
    fragrance
into my lungs. I need no other. I
would spill attar from my eyes,
mix her dust with my salt,
steep my fingers in her stone
and raise them to my lips.

أتأمل تطابق الأصابع .
إنها مسُّ النقود ورنينُها
إذ تهتزُّ في كأس نحاسي ،
إنها النردُ، تبييت الملك ،
طقطقة الخيل على المرمر إذ تلتهم الرخَّ
إنها صخب الدفوف والدربكة
تنهيدةُ الناي وتأملُ القانون ،
إنها شكواكم يا عطار، شكوى أيادي التجار
المحنَّاة بألوان التوابل ،
أما ضحكتها فيغشاها الغبارُ، يا عطّار .

أودَّ لو أشربُه هذا الغبار
أنشَف لساني بهذا الضجيج .
هذه الأزقةُ تصبح ألمًا صحراويًا في حنجرتي ،
وردة شوكية تخرج من أحشائي ،
عطرًا موجعًا في رئتيَّ لا أتعطّر بغيره .
سأسكب العطرَ من عينيَّ يا عطّارْ
أخلط ملحه بغبارها
أخمّر أناملي في حجارتها
وأرفعها إلى شفتيَّ .

AND THEIR LIPS RANG WITH THE SUN

Look at them! Are they not beautiful? Had cinnamon been ground and rubbed into their skin, they could not have been more brown, more fragrant, more beloved of the wine-bright sky.

Come, stranger, come, admire the wealth of our nation, the pride of our city, the joy of our people's eyes. These girls, these women with their slender necks and sloping shoulders, they heft their spears high into the air as they sing the morning up, clash shaft against head in a dawn dance that scatters clouds and rains light on the city below. Hours from now they will lower their weapons and murmur evening down, they will twine forearms and elbows and draw close to each other, brush lash against cheek and embrace before slipping apart to find their seats on the rooftops, curl fists under chins and wait for the morning again. They form a splendid alphabet, do they not? See how swift and clever are their feet, how their lips are sewn with tiny golden bells, how their very breath chimes and shines, the better to spell out the hours of the day in brilliance worthy of the Sun!

It takes a great deal to be worthy of the office.

The girls are chosen to it by the Sun Herself. For the Sun speaks to us in a language all Her own, a language distilled from that which we speak in the streets of the city, hidden within it as wine is hidden in grapes. It is heady, too, and strong: *sheen*, *dah*, *tah*, *noon*, *reh*, *zein*, sounds that brook no spill of liquid before their heat, threaten any lilting sibilance to vapour and smoke if it should come too near. It is a brassy tongue of tambourines and trumpets, and whether born to silk and spice or wool and water, if a girl bears a Sun-letter on her brow at birth she is destined for the rooftops of the temple, for the spear-dance and the song that raises day like a wayward child from its bed.

Would the Sun rise without them? Hah! He asks if the Sun

would rise without them! What a foolish question! But we will forgive you, being new to our land. Have you ever tasted a fig? A pomegranate? You have not until you have tried your teeth against ours. Come into my house; sit down, friend, eat; let this old woman pour you a tea sweet as the sight of our Sun-girls while I tell you about them.

There are always fourteen girls trained to the dawn dance, one for each letter of the Sun's alphabet, and in addition to her morning duties each one must raise her replacement. It happens just often enough: a woman of the town feels the stir of hunger at the stroke of noon, a tugging to a space where she casts no shadow. There she will stand and sweat and munch almonds till her belly's full; weeks later she discovers her belly more full than she anticipated, and she carries the Sun's child. It is sometimes less subtle an affair, but one needn't count back the months to a chancy conception; the letter stamped on newborn skin like a seal is more than lineage enough, and all the name a girl needs.

Thus it is that when Tah finds a child born whose letter matches her own, when Reh sees her name bloom on an infant's ruddy skin, she knows her time has been measured out in the baby's limbs. Once those small hands can hold the spear, once those tender lips can bear the golden bells and breathe them into joyful clamour, then the elder will cede her place, withdraw to the shadows of evening and sing no more.

What happens to them? You ask with such concern! Perhaps you fear to find yourself in a land of savage Barbary, where we slit the throats of our divinities and bake them into savoury pies, eat their death to absorb their life? Dear friend, console yourself; you are in a civilised country, among the learned and the wise. Drink your tea.

When it is time for a Sun-woman to retire—usually at the august age of twenty-eight, having seen her charge to the auspicious age of fourteen—she cedes her place in a beautiful ritual, an intricate dance of twenty-eight interlocking steps that occurs between teacher and apprentice. During the dance, they exchange a total of seven kisses, and after each, the elder sheds one of the seven bells from her lips. A song accompanies the ritual, naturally; it is an astonishing duet, supported by a chorus made up of the other Sun-women. Imagine it: hear how the notes shimmer and change with the exchange of the bells, how the elder's voice rings less and less as the younger's voice gains power and shine! Oh, it is immense, it is a great privilege to behold. Live among us long enough and perhaps you shall be graced with the spectacle.

Ah, of course you are only passing through. Well. That is a pity.

Once the last bell has been hooked into the junior's lips, once the last kiss has been exchanged, the last note sung, the older woman sinks to her knees before her charge, who then puts the tips of her fingers to her elder's temples, thumbs on the letter marking her forehead. She murmurs the name they share. Then there is a fantastic clashing of spear-heads, an ululation in the new letter-bearer's honour, and the younger raises her teacher up and leads her into the heart of the temple, where she will live out the rest of her days in silent service to the Sun. She will light incense in the morning, she will help prepare nourishing meals of lentils and coriander, she will dry yoghurt, roll it into balls, store it in jars of olive oil. She will bake bread. She will light the lamps in the evening, braid the girls' hair as hers was braided in her youth. She may choose to write poetry, secret orisons that the younger girls put to music and sing in the evening. It is a quiet life, and a good one; and when she dies, a day of mourning is declared throughout our land, and her body is burned on a bier of cassis and cinnamon, that her essence may return fragrant and joyful to the Sun.

No. After the ritual, the elders never speak again. It is better that they do not. To hear one's voice sound dull as steamed rice when one is used to years of it gilded in the saffron sound of bells is enough to break one's heart. Bearable, no doubt, but hardly to be wished for. Silence is far easier.

But you asked about the Sun, and whether or not She would rise without the song, and the dance, the bells and the spears chiming together. Let me answer you with a story.

There was once a Sun-woman, glorious as any of them, named Lam. She was nimble, lithe; she was all of eighteen, quite in her prime, while her bright-eyed acolyte had only just learned the sacred alphabet off by heart. She was a sensible teacher, and differed from her sisters in only one respect.

It was her custom, once the dawn-dance was done, to look out to the very farthest reaches of the horizon and imagine how far the fingers of the Rising Sun could reach, what they touched where her gaze failed. And when the evening was shaken out like a sheet between the arms of her sisters, then, too, rather than look to the closing of her palms, she would chase the last ray of the Sun as it vanished over the desert and the mountains, and wonder where She went, where She slept, and in whose bed.

These were unnecessary thoughts for a Sun-woman to have, to be sure, but perhaps none had loved the Sun quite so completely as she.

It happened one afternoon that Lam looked out, as was her wont, towards the west, and wondered. But while she thought her puzzle-thoughts, she became aware of eyes on her, and looked down to the great square before the temple of the Sun.

She saw a hooded stranger, wrapped about in black robes, face covered up to the eyes. But what eyes! Even from so far away, they struck her a blow. She could not, afterwards, have told their colour; only their effect, the shock of them, like wind on wet limbs. They set the hairs of her arms to standing, and she looked away swiftly—when she looked again, the stranger was gone.

Now, perhaps you are thinking you have heard this tale before, have you not? No? There are many versions, it is very well-known, particularly as a cautionary tale: when you feel an eye upon you, you must handle turquoise, make the sign with your fingers to banish evil, like this. You must never, on any account, turn to meet the eye. But so it goes. There would be no tale otherwise, and a tongue without a tale to tell must languish for want of wagging.

Lam thought on the stranger. It was difficult not to, for after the song and the dance and the chiming of the bells, there is precious little to occupy a Sun-woman's thoughts before evening. They are taught to think of the Sun, of Her Rising and Setting, of the many tales told of Her, how she Conquered and Threw Back the Dark of Ages and now wore the Dark as a coverlet, a prize of her Conquest.

Any acolyte could tell you such tales; they are worn smooth as polished cabochon with the telling, passed from mouth to ear like an inheritance of jewels.

No acolyte would tell you of Lam, however. It is not for any Sun-woman to speak of her, and every successor who has borne the letter-name has struggled against its weight like a stone crown on her brow. But I see you grow impatient. No, do not protest; I see you looking for the end of the story in the bottom of your cup, when I have not even reached the middle! Have some more tea; the spice is bracing, it straightens the spine, brightens the eyes.

Lam thought on the stranger. She found herself wondering what was the shape of the mouth beneath the cloth, what colour were the cheeks. She wondered what it would be like to kiss lips unencumbered by bells. She was, it must be said, far too curious for her own good—but even had she been the devoutest of Sun-women, even had she been the most pious, with her thoughts brilliant and unadorned as a bone, she could not have helped but notice that the stranger returned the next afternoon, and the next, and the next. Always to the same place in the great dusty square, to the western side, midway between the temple walls and the first of the city's houses.

Never for more than a moment, never for longer than it took to lock gazes with her. She began to sense that they played a game; sometimes she would look away first, sometimes the stranger would. Always, when she looked back, the stranger would be gone; always, once the stranger turned away, Lam would close her eyes and rest her cheek on her fists, marble-still. She knew that the stranger, too, always looked back to find her withdrawn from the game; she felt that gaze like a pressure against her eyelids before it melted into air and darkness.

The day she felt thoughts of the stranger intrude on the dawn dance, she knew the time had come to do something about it.

It was nothing noticeable to those who woke in time to watch the dance from below; hardly even a misstep, only a lengthening of arc, a dimming of clash when her spear-head met her sister Zein's. Zein noticed, but could hardly point it out, and did not question her afterwards—suppose she had herself been mistaken, what an insult it would have been! No more came of it until that afternoon, when Lam locked eyes with the stranger.

It was the stranger's turn to look away. But when those eyes looked back, Lam held them still, would not release them. She watched as the stranger's eyes widened, watched as the black-clad form stepped back, turned, and walked hurriedly away.

She watched as long as she could.

After the evening lullaby, she waited until her sisters were asleep, stretched and curled along the temple's roof like so many cats. When the last had nodded off, she turned her bells inward, stilled them against her tongue. She took up her spear and leapt nimbly along the flat tops of the city's houses till she found the ground; then she followed the stranger's steps as far as she remembered.

It was strange to be awake when all the city slept. It was stranger still to be so low on the ground, to walk among the houses, beneath the lines strung from wall to wall for washing. It was cold, too, colder than she was used to, and dark as the space between eye and lash.

It was not long before she found herself quite lost.

She wandered from alley to alley, cursing her foolishness, wondering what she had expected—the stranger waiting at the first corner she rounded? She was no hound to seek by scent, couldn't even have said what her stranger smelled like, except the odd mixture of dust and afternoon air she associated with the exchange of their looks. Suppose she found some other bright-eyed wanderer swaddled in dark cloth—what guarantee had she that it would be the one she sought?

She was about to climb a rooftop to gain her bearings and make her way back to the temple, when she heard the song.

It was like the sound of flutes that sometimes reached her from the city's marketplace, like flutes and something else—voices, yes, voices like wind on wet skin. She followed it like an unspooling of thread, winding through the dark alleys till she came to a house smaller and shorter than most, with an odd, domed roof that rose like a pearl onion among the flat tops of the other buildings. There were no lamps lit within; she could see no one. She waited, instead, at the door, listened to the soft chanting that came from inside.

She had never heard anything like it; all liquid and silk, gentle and sad. It unsettled her, rattled strangeness into her thoughts.

As the song wore on, the Moon rose higher in the sky.

She had heard stories spoken of the Moon, sometimes, but found them too outlandish for her taste. What did she care for the lamp lit by the Sun's bedside at night? She was never impressed, either, by the thin, pale crescent she sometimes saw hanging on the ear of evening, the lip of dawn. It seemed confused, lost, out of place in a sky that looked best with the Sun in it.

It did not seem so, now, when she was herself lost. And could that be the Moon, that rose so round and so white, that seemed almost to have a face in it? She had never imagined she could look on something so bright without losing her eyes.

When the song finally ended, her cheeks were wet with tears. She listened still, aching now for more, but all she heard were steps falling like slow rain from within the house, nearing the door.

She hid between the house and its neighbour, listened to the sound of the door opening. She peered around the corner, and froze as one black-clad figure after another stepped out into the street, taking various paths away from the house. She waited till she saw the one she knew to be hers, her stranger, by the cadence of heel falling against earth, the shape of stillness marked out against air.

This is a story, and stories are sometimes more convenient than may be believed. But you must believe me when I tell you that Lam's stranger was the last to leave the house, and by some providence hesitated, paused to adjust veil or robe.

It was then that Lam sprang.

You must believe that she was swift, swift enough to clap hand against mouth and still any cry for help. You must believe that she was strong, too, with muscle firm as the rooftops she danced every morning, and that she wielded her spear as easily as some crook a finger. With its blade at her stranger's neck, she silenced any possibility of protest, ripped hood and veil from the face of her prize, and gasped.

A man stood before her, perhaps some years older than her, skin pale as pearls, eyes the colour of dusty silver. On his forehead was a letter, one of the common letters, the lesser letters, a letter that would never be found above any Sun-girl's eyes.

"Qaf," she said, naming him, spilling her bells from her mouth. They made a sound like coins clunking together, as if rebelling against gilding a sound not beloved of the Sun. She raised a hand to the letter in wonder.

He looked so afraid. He smelled of milk and anise, honey and water. His hair was pale, too, the colour of frankincense bark. But he did not flinch away from her, and when she touched the letter on his skin, he read her own. "Lam," he said, and she had never heard her name so spoken, never heard it without the jangle of bells; it was flutes again, a soft, sweet whistle around the edges of her name, curling a music inside it like colours in abalone.

She stroked his hair, his face. She breathed the strange quiet scent of him. Then she pressed her mouth against his.

I see you blush, friend. Have you a lady at home that would object to your hearing such salaciousness from a foreigner's lips? No, I thought not. Women do not easily brook their men straying far from home for too long, and you, forgive me, have the look of one who is, shall we say, well-travelled. I will not linger overmuch on the details, then, for your delicacy's sake.

But how else to tell you that she felt his teeth with her tongue, and found the shape of them to be hewn differently from her own? How else to say that she gleaned the knowledge of how his teeth made a flute of his breath the way her bells made music of hers? They kissed till she tasted his blood where her bells cut him, till his back warmed the stone she pressed him against, till she knew the shape of his limbs like she knew her alphabet. She pushed him back into the house with the strange domed roof and tore the black from his body, kissed his page-pale skin until she'd inked a scripture of cuts and bruises along it. She bit him and said he tasted of lemon cake; he moaned and said she tasted of cinnamon and cloves. Their love-making was a duet unimagined by troubadour or court composer.

They murmured together, afterwards, of alphabets and language.

He told her how boys born with a Moon-letter on their brows were hidden away for shame, were taken to the small house with its funny dome and left to the charity of the cultists there. He had heard it was different by the sea, where the Moon had mastery over the tides, where the pearl-divers prayed for short days and long nights to soothe their skin from the savage lashing heat—but those, he said sadly, were perhaps only stories told to comfort children who longed to give meaning to a task done in secret to spare it scorn. It did not matter, he told her, that they helped the Moon rise, that they sculpted His shape every night to precise degrees with their songs, guided Him through the perilous tangle of stars that might rip His sweet skin. Had she never seen the blood that appeared on the Moon like a smear of rust when they faltered?

She licked the drying blood on his lips in answer, and he sighed. They slept in each other's arms, lulled by the music of each other's breath.

It was still dark when Lam woke; thick dark, darker than it had been when she found Qaf. The moon must have set, she thought drowsily, and slept more.

When she woke the second time, it was to a great wailing in the streets, and her throat closed with the knowledge of what she had done, what she had failed to do.

The people of the city were weeping. They were striking wooden spoons against copper pots and pans, shouting and shrieking at the sky, lighting torches and shooting flaming arrows into the dark. Children were screaming, burying their heads in their fathers' shirts, asking where had the Sun gone, why had She not Risen, had the Dark of Ages grown again and smothered Her in Her Sleep?

Qaf tried to lead her back to the temple, but the going was difficult, with the clamour and press of so many terrified bodies around them. They clutched each other's hands, but had not gone far when she felt Qaf torn from her; she turned, and Zein was there, staring at her in shocked astonishment. Before Lam could offer a word of explanation, her sister lifted a trumpet to her bell-strung lips and blew into it. How it must have cut her beautiful mouth to do so! Twelve trumpets answered, and Zein took tight hold of Lam's wrist and forced her up to the rooftops, pulled her swiftly towards the temple.

The others were returning as quickly as they could; they had spread out, all of them, in the search. When they saw Lam, they assumed their positions immediately, raised their spears, and began the dance. Lam danced too, of course, tears streaming down her cheeks unchecked, tickling her neck in the places Qaf had kissed her. She had never danced so beautifully, never sung so furiously. She did not miss a step.

The Sun rose like bread, red as sumac, and the people of the city breathed great gulps of relief, sang the song as best they could, wet each other's cheeks with kisses and tears, and went about the business of their day.

Perhaps if Lam had shown any sign of injury, if Qaf had been as vicious with her body as she had been with his, her sisters would have looked at her with less accusation. Perhaps they might have continued to think her stolen away, a victim of the mysterious Dark, returned to them by the Sun's Grace. But she could not lie to them, could not mislead those who knew every twist of ankle, every clench of calf, every exhalation measured to ring her bells. She was part of an alphabet, and in their presence could not help but be read.

The Temple was at a loss. What could they do to punish her? They might have banished her, ripped the bells from her lips, denied her the grace of ceremony and ritual—but Lam's younger namesake was not yet ready to take her place in the dance. They could not risk the younger girl failing, could not risk her training being interrupted. In word, then, all was forgiven; in deed, Lam was closely watched, hardly trusted with the simplest of tasks, shunned by her sisters who drew their lips back in disgust when she drew too near them outside the dance. Even their bells rang contempt at her.

They pitied her, though, when it became clear she was with child.

She danced the dawn-dance every day. Even when her belly grew great as a basket of apples, when her ankles swelled thick as pomegranate trunks, she never missed a step or a note. Her sisters could see what penance she paid, and I believe they forgave her, then.

The city worried about the birth, worried that the Sun would fail again if the dance were delayed for her relief. They needn't have: the Moon is an excellent midwife. When He was round as Lam's belly the pains wracked her, and she wailed and wept like a bird at sea. She was delivered of a boy, they say, skin the colour of milky tea, with the letters of his parents' names joined on his brow. I am told they formed a word: *Qull*, which means "speak" in our language.

Lam never heard him speak more than his first wail. She was not allowed to see him, to hold him. The sisters bathed and swaddled him, and took him to the cultists in their domed house. Their duties, after all, were only the pale reflection of Lam's; perhaps they could better support an infant.

Oh, of course she tried to see him. She had to recover in time for the dawn-dance the next morning, after all; the moment it was done she ran, breasts and belly sagging, to the domed house. None could stop her, though Zein, who loved her best of all her sisters, ran after her. She watched as Lam pounded on the cultists' door, shouted and wept for Qaf, for her son.

The Qaf who opened the door was not hers.

He was scarcely fourteen, just about half her height, but he looked at her with the contempt of an old man. He told her that Qaf—he spat as he spoke his own name—had been banished from their order, and had taken the impure brat with him. They would not sully their temple—as if it could be called that!—by taking in a bastard whelp confused as a sky at sea.

Zein prevented Lam from breaking the flute of his mouth with her fist, but could not stop her from bloodying her knuckles against the door he shut in her face.

And there ends her story.

༄

Why do you frown, friend? It was a long answer to a short question, that I'll admit, and it isn't a tale to shake laughter from the belly, but that is all it is, a tale.

What happened to her? Why, she returned to the temple. She danced the dance every morning, sang the lullaby every evening for nine more years. She yielded her place to her acolyte with all due ceremony.

She sought her son, once. She spent a year searching for Qaf and Qull, froze her dancing feet in the snowy cedar mountains, warmed them again by the matchless sea. She could find no trace of either of them, and returned home—but not to the temple. She would not accept a quiet life of retirement in its service. She felt—quite rightly, I think—that she had given up two lives where most Sun-women gave one, and that she had earned a life outside its walls.

She spoke; she bore the grating of her bell-less voice in her ears as penance until she grew accustomed to its blandness. Even steamed rice grows on one eventually, becomes a familiar sort of comfort. She taught dancing to the common folk, and grew to be a garrulous old woman among them, known for accosting strangers in the square and plying them with more spicy tea than their bladders can comfortably hold. She grew affluent, took the name *Mal*, which means "riches" in our language—

Why, yes. That is indeed what they call me. I see you are a clever lad; here I thought I was being mysterious. No matter. It is a name that serves well enough.

Oh, forgive me! You are right. I never did ask your name. Indulge a forgetful old woman and her dusty manners, and tell it to me now.

Your pardon? I did not hear.

What are you doing? How rude, how dare you unbind your head at an old woman's table? What is that on your—

Oh.

Oh, I see.

It is dreadfully dusty in here, is it not? Gets into the eyes so they can't see themselves in another's face. A moment, please—no, I am all right, I am very well. I am laughing, you see? Only laughing, my dearest heart, my eyes, my breath, my spoken word.

Well—you have a name, you ought to live up to it. Speak, then, please—speak. You must have much to tell me, and I have much rice to feed you, much more tea. And you should know, it was most ungracious of you to lie to me, earlier. I am still strong, you see, still quite strong for my age, and will not hear of your only passing through.

A TALE OF ASH
IN SEVEN BIRDS

We fall as cinders, scattered on the wind. We fall as leaves, a bruising brightness—land lightly on foreign shores, foreign ports, foreign parts. Our shapes unseamed, our mouths untongued, we swallow our burning into new bodies. We break space around our hearts, keep our memories nestled in the hollows of bones built from the outside in.

There is room left over.

The shores, ports, parts, they challenge us to battle. We are weary; we surrender. Nations are great magicians; they pull borders out of hats like knots of silk. *Here*, says the wizard-nation, *here are the terms of a truce: be small, be drab, above all be grateful, and we will let you in.*

We bow our heads, and change.

Sparrow

You keep your head low. You are small, but you are fast; no moment, no movement is wasted. Work, work, work, work, work: forage food, busy yourself with branches, sing in sixty languages the wizard-nation does not understand. The wizard-nation only has one language, and all its words for you are ugly.

You fan the spark in your bones, build your fire, pour it out of you into an egg. But the wizard-nation stalks your nest in cat-shape, grooms itself in studied nonchalance. It wants you small for a reason; wants to fold you into the sac of its stomach, wants to build its muscle from your meat. It chooses its moment.

So do you. As it closes its mouth around you, you hatch from your egg, larger, fiercer, sharper, darker, and croak the wizard-nation's language until it yowls away.

Crow

You suck the light into your feathers, fly fan-tailed into the sun. Your darkness makes the wizard-nation nervous. Because you speak it, the wizard-nation changes its language; it teaches itself to read ill luck in your appearance, teaches itself to despise the gloss of your wings, the sound of your voice. It hates, above all other things, when you speak to other crows: *seven*, it hisses, *for a secret*, and you are not allowed those.

The wizard-nation stalks you in eagle-shape; it flies above you, keeps you in its shadow until you lose all sense of the sun. But there is water beneath you, and outwith the eagle's shadow are sparks that remind you of being born.

Angling its wings, the wizard-nation swoops in to hang you on its talons' hooks.

You breathe deep, sleek your feathers, furl your wings tight against your body, and dive.

Cormorant

The shoreline is a difficult place.

It, like you, is many things at once: a border blurred, a body ambiguous. You swim, you fly, you walk along it; you skirt its dangers, feed mostly on fish. Your diet is varied because you are always hungry. You never take more than you need.

With each dive you bite the river bottom, carry mud in your beak, break the surface. You try, where you can, to build beaches: bit by bit, a place to rest, a place to nest, a place the wizard-nation can't drive you from.

You make an island. Saplings grow on it, bind the mud together with roots. Here is a home, now, for gulls and ducks and sandpipers, creatures who are many things at once, whose languages are amphibious.

The wizard-nation is furious. It stalks you in raccoon-shape, makes meals of your eggs. You cannot nest safely; you dare not hatch chicks, though the spark of you burns, flickers, longs to spread and give heat and light. The raccoon washes its hands in the river while watching you, for the wizard-nation is nothing if not fastidious, is nothing if not next to godliness.

When you are wearied and miserable, when your neighbours have all fled the wizard-nation's teeth, you feel the raccoon's shadow smother your own. In the seconds before it tears feather from flesh, you fold yourself inward, swallow your languages, turn yourself inside out.

Swallow

Your tail scissors ribbons from the sky. You remember mud and roots, build sturdy clay nests. You are dark above and bright below, and you wear your spark in iridescence. You are fierce in flight, swift and agile, and you are a knife defending your eggs, swoop and sweep unflinching into faces, strike fear into your foes. Your wings are scimitars. You will keep your children safe.

The wizard-nation stalks you in cuckoo-shape.

It mimics doughty sparrowhawks, throws its voice, sows confusion among your kind. While you fight the air, search for eagles to mob, the wizard-nation slips into your nest.

Did you lay that mottled egg, you wonder? Could such a thing have come from you? But it is in your nest, and you must protect it, you must hatch it, and when you do the wizard-nation mewls for your protection and succour. *Me*, it says, *look at me, love me, give everything to me and I will love you back*, while it thrashes and smashes your eggs to bits.

Your heart breaks with them, and you change.

Hummingbird

You split your tongue in two. You learn to fly backwards as well as forwards, straight up and down—you can stand on anything, even air. You have made yourself small and fast, and your eggs are tiny, your nest too small for a cuckoo to hide inside. Your mouth is a needle and a sword. You shine, still.

And the wizard-nation seems to love you, now, at last. Perhaps you have found the right balance of beauty and fierceness, size and speed? You are at home anywhere, you cannot be said to take anything from other birds, for you have learned to drink strength from flowers.

The wizard-nation stalks you in mantis-shape.

The wizard-nation is pious. The wizard-nation is holy. The wizard-nation makes a flower out of the dead bodies of ancient creatures and fills it with red sweetness for your sake.

The wizard-nation stands still, lies in wait.

When you see the flower you think, how generous. When you see the flower you think, how kind. You approach the flower to sip—hardly even out of hunger, but out of deep, genuine gratitude for this gift, this effort expended on your behalf—bend your head to the bloom.

The mantis preys. Its arms fall like scythes into the flesh of your impossibly small bright body. It stills the throbbing shimmer of your wings. It pulls you close enough to kiss.

You are so, so tired of being eaten.

You stab your beak through the wizard-nation's face, and change.

Great Horned Owl

You are an apex predator. Nothing can hurt you now.

You have embraced silence. Your wings make no sound. Language is for prey, for what the wizard-nation hunts. You are not prey, not anymore.

Sparrows, though. Crows. Cormorants. All these will fill your belly now, and it's their own fault. All their own fault for not choosing a shape the wizard-nation cannot hurt, their own fault for being small or loud or trying to build communities of which the wizard-nation disapproves. You have learned the wizard-nation's way, and you will be able to stay, now, forever.

You are an indifferent parent. You lay eggs; some will hatch. You never look too closely at the results. Sometimes you eat them too.

The wizard-nation stalks you in fire-shape.

Small things catch at first. Dry leaves. Tall grasses. Then twigs; then bark. Animals scamper through the undergrowth and scream.

You think, but I am become like the wizard-nation. You think, what shape has it taken to hunt itself, to break itself? What shape is this that, finally, spells the wizard-nation's end?

You smell burning and remember being a spark. You smell smoke and cough and remember falling as cinders, scattered on the wind. You breathe pain.

You set yourself on fire, and change.

Phoenix

We rise and our wings are flame. We rise and our food is air. We rise and we are heat, and we are light, and we are dark and we are bright, and we lick the wind with our thousand fiery tongues. We rise from the wizard-nation's wreck.

We are magnificent.

We seed the sky with embers. And still we rise, we onyx, rubies, garnets, constellate in burning jewels. *There is the Hunter, there the Bird.*

We nest in renewal.

We may fall as cinders, scattered on the wind. We may fall as leaves, a bruising brightness. Or we may not.

Death is a memory we keep in the broken space around our hearts.

There is always room left over.

QAHR

for Bisan

They are doing all these things to destroy the depth of us . . . what does it mean, Qahr—Qahr, is to make someone—so sad—I don't know what it means in English, I don't know. But they're trying to Qahr us.
                                            —Bisan Owda

Qahr: a collapse. A caving in
of the chest, a hollowing,
a lit match burning in a stoppered bottle
til the cork's sucked in by void. Qahr,
a stone in the mouth on fire, a coal
swallowed whole and searing,
crushed slag in the throat.

they are doing all these things to destroy the depth of us

Qahr, yaani—yaani shou? Bisan,
I never learned this word. Children shouldn't, and I was a
    child,
six or seven, when I stopped learning our language. Qahr
hid in my parents' hands, my grandmother's voice,
while I learned to rhyme "leaf" with "brief"—learned
to catch lizards and chase chickens, to be told
that I spoke like a foreigner.

I am learning now, from children.

قهر

إلى بيسان

إنهم يقومون بكل هذا لتدمير أعماقنا. ما القهر؟ القهر هو أن تجعل إنسانًا يشعر بحزن لا يوصف. لا أعرف لها معنى بالإنجليزية، ولكنهم يحاولون قهرنا.
—بيسان عودة

القهرُ: انهيارٌ، خَسْفٌ في الصدر، فجوةٌ،
عودُ ثقاب مشتعلٌ في قارورةٍ محكمةٍ
يبتلعُ الفراغُ سدَّتَها.
القهرُ، حجرٌ في الفم، مشتعلٌ،
ابتلاع جمرة كاوية بأكملها،
إنه خَبَثٌ مسحوقٌ في الحلق.

إنهم يقومون بكل هذا لتدمير أعماقنا.

القهر، يعني ... يعني شو؟
بيسان، أنا لم أتعلم هذه الكلمة من قبل،
ولا ينبغي ان يتعرض الأطفال لها.
كنتُ طفلة، ابنة ست سنوات، سبعًا،
حين توقفت عن تعلّم لغتنا،
حين خبّأ والديَّ القهرَ في أيديهما،
وحبسته جدَّتي في صوتها،
حين بدأتُ برصف القوافي،
حين تعلمت اصطياد السحالي ومطاردة الدجاج،
حين قالوا لي إنني أتكلم كأجنبية.

الآن أتعلّم من الأطفال.

I am learning, Qahr
is when my mother says she can't function
until she wraps a keffiyeh around her head. Qahr
is the cratering in my heart that spreads
like ink devouring the page,

when I see a boy,
so small, six or seven,
outraged, crying,
reach for his dead father, calling
baba, baba, baba
as if he could wake him,
as if the world made sense,
as if a single word in any language
could hold all this wrecking grief.

أتعلّم أن القهر حين تقولُ أمي
إنها لا تستطيع عملاً إن لم تَتَبَلسَمْ بكوفيتِها.
القهر، فَوْهة في قلبي
تتمدد كبقعة حبرٍ تلتهم بياض الصفحة،

حين أرى صبيًا، في عمرٍ نَديٍّ،
ستُ سنوات، سبعٍ،
يتلظّى، يصرخ،
يحاول الوصول إلى والده القتيل،
ينادي،
بابا، بابا، بابا
لعلّه يوقظه،
كأنما العالمُ ما زال عاقلا،
كأنما كلمةٌ ما، في لغةٍ ما،
تتسع لهذا الحزن المدمّر.

THE TRUTH ABOUT OWLS

Owls have eyes that match the skies they hunt through. Amber-eyed owls hunt at dawn or dusk; golden-eyed owls hunt during the day; black-eyed owls hunt at night.

No one knows why this is.

Anisa's eyes are black, and she no longer hates them. She used to wish for eyes the colour of her father's, the beautiful pale green-blue that people were always startled to see in a brown face. But she likes, now, having eyes and hair of a colour those same people find frightening.

Even her teachers are disconcerted, she's found—they don't try to herd her as they do the other students. She sees them casting uncertain glances towards her before ushering their group from one owl exhibit to another, following the guide. She turns to go in the opposite direction. "Annie-sa! Annie, this way!"

She turns, teeth clenching. Mrs. Roberts, whose pale powdered face, upswept yellow hair, and bright red lips make Anisa think of Victoria sponge, is smiling encouragingly.

"My name is A-NEE-sa, actually," she replies, and feels the power twitching out from her chest and into her arms, which she crosses quickly, and her hands, which she makes into fists, digging nails into her palms. The power recedes, but she can still feel it pouring out from her eyes like a swarm of bees while Mrs. Roberts looks at her in perplexed confusion. Mrs. Roberts' eyes are a delicate, ceramic sort of blue.

Anisa watches another teacher, Ms. Grewar, lean over to murmur something into Mrs. Roberts' ear. Mrs. Roberts only looks more confused, but renews her smile uncertainly, nods, and turns back to her group. Anisa closes her eyes, takes a deep breath, and counts to ten before walking away.

༄

Owls are predators. There are owls that would tear you apart if you gave them half a chance.

༄

The Scottish Owl Centre is a popular destination for school trips: a short bus ride from Glasgow, an educational component, lots of opportunities for photographs to show the parents, and who doesn't like owls nowadays? Anisa has found herself staring, more than once, at owl-print bags and shirts, owl-shaped earrings and belt buckles, plush owl toys and wire statues in bright, friendly colours. She finds it all desperately strange.

Anisa remembers the first time she saw an owl. She was seven years old. She lived in Riyaq with her father and her grandparents, and that morning she had thrown a tantrum about having to feed the chickens, which she hated, because of their smell and the way they pecked at her when she went to gather their eggs, and also because of the rooster, who was fierce and sharp-spurred. She hated the chickens, she shouted, why didn't they just make them into soup.

She was given more chores to do, which she did, fumingly, stomping her feet and banging cupboard doors and sometimes crying about how unfair it was. "Are you brooding over the chickens," her father would joke, trying to get her to laugh, which only made her more furious, because she *did* want to laugh but she didn't want him to think she wasn't still mad, because she was.

She had calmed down by lunch, and forgotten about it by supper. But while helping her grandmother with the washing up she heard a scream from the yard. Her grandmother darted out, and Anisa followed, her hands dripping soap.

An owl—enormous, tall as a lamb, taller than any bird she had ever seen—perched in the orange tree, the rooster a tangle of blood and feathers in its talons. As Anisa stared, the owl bent its head to the rooster's throat and tore out a long strip of flesh.

When Anisa thinks about this—and she does, often, whenever her hands are wet and soapy in just the right way, fingertips on the brink of wrinkling—she remembers the guilt. She remembers listening to her grandmother cross herself and speak her words of protection against harm, warding them against death in the family, against troubled times. She remembers the fear, staring at the red and pink and green of the rooster, its broken, dangling head.

But she can't remember—though she often tries—whether she felt, for the first time, the awful electric prickle of the power in her chest, flooding out to her palms.

※

There are owls that sail through the air like great ships. There are owls that flit like finches from branch to branch. There are owls that look at you with disdain and owls that sway on the perch of your arm like a reed in the wind.

※

Anisa is not afraid of owls. She thinks they're interesting enough, when people aren't cooing over them or embroidering them onto cushions. From walking around the sanctuary she thinks the owl she saw as a child was probably a Eurasian eagle owl.

She wanders from cage to cage, environment to environment, looking at owls that bear no resemblance to the pretty patterns lining the hems of skirts and dresses—owls that lack a facial disk, owls with bulging eyes and fuzzy heads, owls the size of her palm.

Some of the owls have names distinct from their species: Hosking, Broo, Sarabi. Anisa pauses in front of a barn owl and frowns at the name. Blodeuwedd?

"Blow-due-wed," she sounds out beneath her breath, while the owl watches her.

"It's Bloh-DA-weth, actually," says a friendly voice behind her. Anisa turns to see one of the owl handlers from the flying display, a Black woman named Izzy, hair wrapped up in a brightly coloured scarf, moving into one of the aviaries, gloved hands clutching a feed bucket. "It means 'flower-face' in Welsh."

Anisa flushes. She looks at the owl again. She has never seen a barn owl up close, and does not think it looks like flowers; she thinks, all at the same time, that the heart-shaped face is alien and eerie and beautiful and like when you can see the moon while the sun is setting, and that there should be a single word for the colour of the wings that's like the sheen of a pearl but not the pearl itself.

She asks, "Is it a boy or a girl?"

"Do you not know the story of Blodeuwedd?" Izzy smiles. "She was a beautiful woman, made of flowers, who was turned into an owl."

Anisa frowns. "That doesn't make sense."

"It's from a book of fairy tales called *The Mabinogion*—not big on sensemaking." Izzy chuckles. "I don't think she likes it either, to be honest. She's one of our most difficult birds. But she came to us from Wales, so we gave her a Welsh name."

Anisa looks into Blodeuwedd's eyes. They are blacker than her own.

"I like her," she declares.

A group of owls is called a parliament. Owls are bad luck.

The summer Anisa saw the owl kill the rooster was the summer Israel bombed the country. She always thinks of it that way, not as a war—she doesn't remember a war. She never saw anyone fighting. She remembers a sound she felt more than heard, a *thud* that shook the earth and rattled up through her bones—then another—then a smell like chalk—before being swept into her father's arms and taken down into shelter.

She remembers feeling cold; she remembers, afterwards, anger, weeping, conversations half-heard from her bed, her mother's voice reaching them in sobs from London, robotic and strangled over a poor internet connection, a mixing of English and Arabic, accents swapping places. Her father's voice always calm, measured, but with a tension running through it like when her cousin put a wire through a dead frog's leg to make it twitch.

She remembers asking her grandmother if Israel attacked

because of the owl. Her grandmother laughed in a way that made Anisa feel hollow and lost.

"Shh, shh, don't tell Israel! An owl killed a rooster—that's more reason to attack! An owl killed a rooster in Lebanon and the government let it happen! Quick, get off the bridges!"

The whole family laughed. Anisa was terrified, and told no one.

Why did the owl not go courting in the rain? Because it was too wet to woo.

"What makes her 'difficult'?" asks Anisa, watching Blodeuwedd sway on her perch. Izzy looks fondly at the owl.

"Well, we acquired her as a potential display bird, but she just doesn't take well to training—she hisses at most of the handlers when they pass by, tries to bite. She's also very territorial, and won't tolerate the presence of male birds, so we can't use her for breeding." Izzy offers Blodeuwedd a strip of raw chicken, which she gulps down serenely.

"But she likes you," Anisa observes. Izzy smiles ruefully.

"I'm not one of her trainers. It's easy to like people who ask nothing of you." Izzy pauses, eyes Blodeuwedd with exaggerated care. "Or at least, it's easy to not hate them."

Before Anisa leaves with the rest of her class, Izzy writes down *Mabinogion* for her on a piece of paper, a rather deft doodle of an owl's face inside a five-petaled flower, and an invitation to come again.

Most owls are sexually dimorphic: the female is usually larger, stronger, and more brightly coloured than the male.

Anisa's mother is tall, and fair, and Anisa looks nothing like her. Her mother's brown hair is light and thin and straight; her mother's skin is pale. Anisa is used to people making assumptions—*are you adopted? Is that your stepmother?*—when they see them together, but her mother's new job at the university has made outings together rare. In fact, since moving to Glasgow, Anisa hardly sees her at home anymore, since she has evening classes and departmental responsibilities.

"What are you reading?" asks her mother, shrugging on her coat after a hurried dinner together.

Anisa, legs folded up underneath her on the couch, holds up a library copy of *The Mabinogion*. Her mother looks confused, but nods, wishes her a good night, and leaves.

Anisa reads about how Math, son of Mathonwy, gathered the blossoms of oak, of broom, of meadowsweet, and shaped them into a woman. She wonders, idly, what kinds of flowers could be combined to make her.

There are owls on every continent in the world except Antarctica.

The so-called war lasted just over a month; Anisa learned the word "ceasefire" in August. Her father put her on a plane to London the moment the airports were repaired.

Before Anisa started going to school, her mother took her aside. "When people ask you where you're from," she told her, "you say 'England,' all right? You were born here. You have every bit as much right to be here as anyone else."

"Baba wasn't born here." She felt a stinging in her throat and eyes, a pain of *unfair*. "Is that why he's not here? Is he not allowed to come?"

Anisa doesn't remember what her mother said. She must have said something. Whatever it was, it was certainly not that she wouldn't see her father in person for three years.

The Welsh word for owl once meant "flower-face."

When Izzy said Blodeuwedd was made of flowers, Anisa had imagined roses and lilies, flowers she was forced to read about over and over in books of English literature. But as she reads, she finds that even Blodeuwedd's flower names are strange to her—what kind of a flower is "broom"?—and she likes that, likes that no part of Blodeuwedd is familiar or expected.

Anisa has started teaching herself Welsh, mostly because she wants to know how all the names in *The Mabinogion* are pronounced. She likes that there is a language that looks like English but sounds like Arabic; she likes that there is no one teaching it to her, or commenting on her accent, or asking her how to speak it for their amusement. She likes that a single "f" is pronounced "v," that "w" is a vowel—likes that it's an alphabet of secrets hidden in plain sight.

She starts visiting the owl centre every weekend, feeling like she's done her homework if she can share a new bit of *Mabinogion* trivia with Izzy and Blodeuwedd in exchange for a fact about owls.

༶

Owls are birds of the order Strigiformes, *a word derived from the Latin for "witch."*

༶

During Anisa's first year of school in England a girl with freckles and yellow hair leaned over to her while the teacher's back was turned, and asked if her father was dead.

"No!" Anisa stared at her.

"My mum said your dad could be dead. Because of the war. Because there's always war where you're from."

"That's not true."

The freckled girl narrowed her eyes. "My mum *said* so."

Anisa felt her pulse quicken, her hands tremble. She felt she had never hated anyone in her whole life so much as this idiot pastry of a girl. She watched as the girl shrugged and turned away.

"Maybe you just don't understand English."

She felt something uncoil inside her. Anisa stood up from her chair and *shoved* the girl out of hers, and felt, in the moment of skin touching skin, a startling shock of static electricity; the girl's freckles vanished into the pink of her cheeks, and instead of protesting the push, she shouted, "Ugh, she *shocked* me!"

In her memory, the teacher's reprimand, the consequences, the rest of that year all melt away to one viciously satisfying image: the freckled girl's blue eyes looking at her, terrified, out of a pretty pink face.

She learned to cultivate an appearance of danger, of threat; she learned that with an economy of look, of gesture, of insinuation, she could be feared and left alone. She was the Girl Who Came From War, the Girl Whose Father Was Dead, the Girl With Powers. One day a boy tried to kiss her; she pushed him away, looked him in the eye, and flung a fistful of nothing at him, a spray of air. He was absent from school for two days; when the boy came back claiming to have had a cold, everyone acknowledged Anisa as the cause. When some students asked her to make them sick on purpose, to miss an exam or assignment, she smirked, said nothing, and walked away.

Owls have a narrow field of binocular vision; they compensate for this by rotating their heads up to 270 degrees.

Carefully, Izzy lowers her arm to Anisa's gloved wrist, hooks her tether to the ring dangling from it, and watches as Blodeuwedd hops casually down onto her forearm. Anisa exhales, then grins. Izzy grins back.

"I can't believe how much she's mellowed out. She's really surprisingly comfortable with you."

"Maybe," Anisa says, mischievous, "it's because I'm really good at not asking anything of her."

"Sure," says Izzy, "or maybe it's because you keep talking about how much you hate Math, son of Mathonwy."

"Augh, that *prick*!"

Izzy laughs, and Anisa loves to hear her, to see how she tosses her head back when she does. She loves how thick and wiry Izzy's hair is, and the different things she does with it—today it's half wrapped in a white and purple scarf, fluffed out at the back like a bouquet. She continues, "He's the worst. He takes flowers and tells them to be a woman; as soon as she acts in a way he doesn't like, he turns her into an owl. It's like—he needs to keep being in charge of her story, and the way to do that is to change her shape."

"Well. To be fair. She did try to kill his adopted son."

"He forced her into marriage with him! And he was a jerk too!"

"You're well into this, you are."

"It's just—" Anisa bites her lip, looking at Blodeuwedd, raising her slightly to shift the weight on her forearm, watching her spread her magnificent wings, then settle. "—sometimes . . . I feel like I'm just a collection of bits of things that someone brought together at random and called *girl*, and then *Anisa*, and then . . ." She shrugs. "Whatever."

Izzy is quiet for a moment. Then she says, thoughtfully, "You know, there's another word for that."

"For what?"

"What you just described—an aggregation of disparate things. An anthology. That's what *The Mabinogion* is, after all."

Anisa is unconvinced. "Blodeuwedd's just one part of someone else's story, she's not an anthology herself."

Izzy smiles, with a gentleness that always makes Anisa feel she's thinking of someone or something else, but allowing Anisa a window's worth of view into her world. "You can look at it that way. But there's another word for anthology, one we don't really use anymore: 'florilegium.' Do you know what it means?"

Anisa shakes her head, and blinks, startled, as Blodeuwedd does a sidewise walk up her arm to lean, gently, against her shoulder. Izzy smiles, a little more brightly, more for her, and says: "A gathering of flowers."

Owls fly more silently than any other bird.

When her father joined them in London three years later, he found Anisa grown several inches taller and several sentences shorter. Her mother's insistence on speaking Arabic together at all times—pushing her abilities as a heritage speaker to their limits—meant that Anisa often chose not to speak at all. This was to her advantage in the school yard, where her eyes, her looks, and rumours of her dark powers held her fellow students in awe; it did her no good with her father, who hugged her and held her until words and tears gushed out of her in gasps.

The next few years were better; they moved to a different part of the city, and Anisa was able to make friends in a new school, to open up, to speak. She sometimes told stories about how afraid of her people used to be, how she'd convinced them of her powers like it was a joke on them, and not something she had ever believed herself.

Owls purge from themselves the matter they cannot absorb: bones, fur, claws, teeth, feathers.

"Is that for school?"

Anisa looks up from her notebook to her mother, and shakes her head. "No. It's Welsh stuff."

"Oh." Her mother pauses, and Anisa can see her mentally donning the gloves with which to handle her. "Why Welsh?"

She shrugs. "I like it." Then, seeing her mother unsatisfied, adds, "I like the stories. I'd like to read them in the original language eventually."

Her mother hesitates. "You know, there's a rich tradition of Arabic storytelling—"

The power flexes inside her like a whip snapping, takes her by surprise, and she bites the inside of her lip until it bleeds to stop it, stop it.

"—and I know I can't share much myself but I'm sure your grandmother or your aunt would love to talk to you about it—"

Anisa grabs her books and runs to her room as if she could

outrun the power, locks the door, and buries her fingernails in the skin of her arms, dragging long, painful scratches down them, because the only way to let the power out is through pain, because if she doesn't hurt herself she knows with absolute certainty that she will hurt someone else.

Illness in owls is difficult to detect and diagnose until it is dangerously advanced.

Anisa knows something is wrong before she sees the empty cage, from the way Izzy hovers in front of it, as if waiting for her.

"Blodeuwedd's sick," she says, and Anisa feels a rush of gravity inside her stomach. "She hasn't eaten in a few days. I'm sorry, but you won't be able to see her—"

"What's wrong with her?" Anisa begins counting back the days to the last flare, to what she thought about, and it wasn't this, it was never anything like this, but she'd held *The Mabinogion* in her hands—

"We don't know yet. I'm so sorry you came out all this way—" Izzy hesitates while Anisa stands, frozen, feeling herself vanishing into misery, into a day one year and four hundred miles away.

Owls do not mate for life, though death sometimes parts them.

The memory is like a trap, a steel cage that falls over her head and severs her from reality. When the memory descends she can do nothing but see her father's face, over and over, aghast, more hurt than she has ever seen him, and her own words like a bludgeon to beat in her own head: "Fine, go back and *die*, I don't care, just *stop coming back*."

She feels, again, the power lashing out, confused, attempting both to tether and to push away; she remembers the shape of the door knob in her hand as she bolts out of the flat, down the stairs, out the building, into the night. She feels incandescent, too burnt up to cry, thinking of her father going back to a country every day in the news, every day a patchwork of explosions and body counts, every day a matter of someone else's opinions.

She thinks of how he wouldn't take her with him.

And she feels, irrevocably, as if she is breathing a stone when she sees him later that evening in hospital, eyes closed, ashen, and the words reaching her from a faraway dimness saying he has suffered a stroke, and died.

"Anisa—A*ni*sa!" Izzy has taken her hands, is holding them, and when Anisa focuses again she feels as if they're submerged in water, and she wants to snatch them away because what if she hurts Izzy but she is disoriented and before she knows what she is doing she is crying while Izzy holds her hands and sinks down to the rain-wet floor with her. She feels gravel beneath her knees and grinds them deeper into it, to punish herself for this, this thing, the power, and she is trying to make Izzy understand and she is trying to say she is sorry but all that comes out is this violent, wrecking weeping.

"It's me," she manages, "I made her sick, it's my fault, I don't mean to do it but I make bad things happen just by wanting them even a little, wanting them the wrong way, and I don't want it anymore, I never wanted *this* but it keeps happening and now she'll die—"

Izzy looks at her, squeezes her hands, and says, calm and even, "Bullshit."

"It's true—"

"Anisa—if it's true it should work both ways. Can you make good things happen by wanting them?"

She looks into Izzy's warm dark eyes, at a loss, and can't frame a reply to such a ridiculous question.

"Think, pet—what *good* things do you want to happen?"

"I want . . ." She closes her eyes, and bites her lip, looking for pain to quash the power but feels it differently—feels, with Izzy holding her hands, Izzy facing her, grounded, as if draining something out into the gravel and the earth beneath it and leaving something else in its wake, something shining and slick as sunlight on wet streets. "I want Blodeuwedd to get better. I want her to have a good life, to . . . be whatever she wants to be and do whatever she wants to do. I want to learn Welsh. I want to—" Izzy's face shimmers through her tears. "I want to be friends with you. I want—"

She swallows them down, all of her good wants, how much she misses her father and how much she misses just talking, in any language, with her mother, and how she misses the light in Riyaq and the dry dusty air, the sheep and the goats and the warmth, always, of her grandmother and uncles and aunts and cousins all around, and she makes an anthology of them. She gathers the flowers of her wants all together in her throat, her heart, her belly, and trusts that they are good.

The truth about owls—

Anisa and her mother stand at the owl centre's entrance, both casually studying a nearby freezer full of ice lollies while waiting for their tickets. Their eyes meet, and they grin at each other. Her mother is rummaging about for caramel Cornettos when the sales attendant, Rachel, waves Anisa over.

"Is that your mother, Anisa?" whispers Rachel. Anisa goes very still for a moment as she nods, and Rachel beams. "I thought so. You have precisely the same smile."

Anisa blushes, and looks down, suddenly shy. Her mother pays for their tickets and ice cream, and together they move towards the gift shop and the aviaries beyond.

Anisa pauses on her way through the gift shop; she waves her mother on, says she'll catch her up. Alone, she buys a twee notebook covered in shiny metallic owls and starts writing in it with an owl-topped pen.

She writes "The truth about owls—" but pauses. She looks at the words, their shape, the taken-for-granted ease of their spilling from her. She frowns, bites her lip, and after a moment's careful thought writes "Y gwir am tylluanod—"

But she has run out of vocabulary, and this is not something she wants to look up. There is a warmth blossoming in her, a rightness, pushing up out of her chest where the power used to crouch, where something lives now that is different, better, and she wants to pour that out on the page. She rolls the pen between her thumb and forefinger, then shifts the journal's weight against her palm.

She writes ان الحقيقة عن البوم معقدة and smiles.

WING

In a café lit by morning, a girl with a book around her neck sits quietly at a table.

She reads—not the book around her neck, which is small, only as long and as wide as her thumb, black cord threaded through a sewn leather spine, knotted shut. She reads a book of maps and women, turns every page as if it were a lock of hair, gently. Every so often, her fingers stray to the book that sits above her sternum, twist it one way, then the other; every so often, she sips her tea.

"What is written in your book?" asks the man who brought her the tea. She looks up.

It is said, she reads, *that a map drawn on a virgin's skin creates a land on the other side of the moon. Whole civilisations rise, whole empires are built in the time it takes for bath water and scented soap to tear its minarets down, smash its aqueducts, strike its flying machines from the star-sewn sky. This is likely nonsense, but as no one has been to the other side of the moon, it remains entirely possible.*

The man blushes, then frowns. "That's nice," he says, "but I meant in *your* book. The one you wear. What is written there?"

The girl's lashes touch her cheeks. "A secret."

He opens his mouth to ask another question, then shuts it. He walks away.

The girl with the book around her neck sits quietly beneath a chestnut tree.

She reads a book with a halved pomegranate on the cover, a wasp stamping its black feet in the juice. She turns every page as if she were lifting a veil, delicately. The sun is bright against the paper, makes the words swim green against her eyes.

Another girl comes by, her hair curly, her step light. She wears a bag over one shoulder, and sits down near the girl with the book around her neck. She smiles. The girl with the book around her neck smiles back. The girl with the bag pulls out a loaf of bread, a wedge of cheese, a small jar of amber honey, and a knife; she begins to slice, to pair cheese slices with apple slices, to drizzle honey on the lot.

"What are you reading?" she asks, curious.

Once, reads the girl, *only once, for never has this happened since, nor is it likely to, a bird lit down on the head of a young man seated beneath a peach tree. The bird's plumage was most fine, smooth as linen, bright as the afternoon sun drinking garden petals. The man could not gaze at it, but sat very still, so as not to disturb it; he closed his eyes, for even the barest flash of tail or pinion as it shifted about his scalp was painful to him, was too beautiful for his gaze. The bird whispered in his ear the secret to immortality, which involved the consumption of nectar, the building of a fire, and the bathing of his limbs in a sacred pool. So deep was the young man's gratitude, so fierce was his love for the beautiful creature perched on his head, that his heart burst in his chest and he died on the spot.*

The girl with the bag, who had begun to chew her honeyed cheese and bread, coughs a little as she laughs. She wipes her mouth modestly and offers the girl with the book around her neck a morsel of her own. She accepts it, and they munch together in silence. Then, as they are rubbing their fingers together to clean the honey from them, the girl with the bag asks, "What is written in the book around your neck?"

She blushes. "A secret."

"Oh," says the other girl. They spend a few more moments together, before the girl with the bag gathers up her effects, bids the girl with the book around her neck a kind farewell, and goes on her way.

The girl with the book around her neck sits quietly on a jutting rock by the sea.

The sea is not quiet; the sea is an angry choir of dissonant voices, all taking turns striking their rage against the shore. The waves curl foamy fingers towards the rocks, smash their delicate salt bones to glass. Everywhere is a fine damp mist.

The girl has no book to hand. She pulls back the left sleeve of her raincoat, dips her fingers into a tidal pool, lifts a mixture of sand and clay from it, and tries to draw a map on her skin.

It is not thick enough; the wet sand will not make lines, only prickle her as it winds its way along her forearm. She pulls her sleeve back down. She looks out at the sea, at the gulls mewling, the crows cawing, and tries to think of a song.

A boy approaches the rock on which she sits. He looks up at her. She looks down at him.

He wears a raincoat too, grey as the sea, and a dark blue scarf around his neck to keep the damp from his throat. It is sensible; she does the same. They look at each other a long moment.

Then he says, "Would you like to hear a story?"

She nods.

"It is said that once every five hundred and sixty-three days, two people will walk on the beach with matching raincoats. It is further said that every one thousand one hundred and twenty-six days, these people will have matching shoes. But it is rare as a bird with feathers linen-smooth, rare as a city on the dark side of the moon, that they will both wear books around their necks, and rarer still that those books will hold secrets."

"Come up," whispers the girl to the boy with a book around his neck. "Come up here."

He does, with his hands to the rock, his shoes like hers, his coat like hers. He unbuttons the collar, unwinds the scarf from his neck. There is a book there, the same length and width as hers, black cord threaded through its sewn leather spine, knotted shut. He reaches for the knot with slender fingers.

"Wait," she says, "wait." She unbuttons her collar, unwinds her scarf, bares her own book for the opening, bites her lip as she looks at him. "Are you sure?"

"I want to tell you a secret," he says, firm.

They open their books. They turn every page as if touching each other's cheeks. They read the same word, the only word, buried in each book's deepest heart, nestled up against its sewn leather spine, behind its knotted ribs.

When the tide comes in, it finds a clutch of soft grey feathers sticking to the rocks, spilling from the pages of two tiny books with no words in them. The tide yawns; it licks them like a cat; it tangles the black cord that threads them, knots them together, and swallows them into the sea.

A HOLLOW PLAY

Dear Paige,

I'm heading out of the flat tonight, for once, since Anna invited me out to a cabaret thing. Funny how it happened—for weeks she's been casually asking what I'm doing after work, but never following up after I say some variation on "derby practice" or "watching cartoons." I guess it's taken her until now to decide I'm someone she'd actually choose to hang out with in her free time. That should make me feel good, right? But I'm actually terrified. Because it's been so long since—I don't know, since I've had a friend? That sounds horrible. And it's probably not true, if I sit and think about it properly. What I mean is, since I've had a friend the way I had friends in Canada. When it was easy, you know? When I could click with someone and just feel this trust, this knowledge that we both liked each other equally and in the same way, when I could take for granted that I could say things and have them be understood. Like with you. It feels like forever since I've had that. A year, at least.

So anyway, I feel like I might have that with Anna—but we're always at work, and all the conversations we have are sandwiched between people ordering flat whites and the occasional biscuit. When it gets quiet, though, sometimes we really talk, about serious things, heart things. I've told her a bit about you. She told me she's trans—which isn't a secret, it's okay that I'm telling you—and we talked about how basically we're both always coming out, we can never be wholly done coming out.

I guess I'm terrified of messing this up somehow. Being boring. Not being into the show that she's really excited about. Being—yeah, okay, being an obnoxious North American in the company of British people, even though Glasgow's about a million times better than London for not making me feel that way.

Right, it's time to go. I'll write more later.

Love,
Emily

Emily stood in the doorway to the Rio Cafe and looked around, half-convinced she had the wrong place. The word "cabaret" had conjured up visions of illicit underground doings populated by white-faced pianists in dark, shabby suits, coaxing notes of tragic joy from their instruments. But this was just a really nice pub, full of comfortable, brightly coloured wooden booths perpendicular to a long bar. There were some smaller tables and chairs to the right and back of it, blackboards with specials written on them, and nothing that looked like it could be turned into a stage.

Make sure you get there early, Anna had said, *it fills up fast*. Emily shrugged, manoeuvred her way to one of the small tables towards the back, pulled a pen and a leather-bound journal from her bag, and resumed writing.

Dear Paige,

So, I'm here, but Anna's not, and I awesomely left Memoirs of a Spacewoman *at home in spite of knowing I'd have two hours to kill, so I figure I'll just keep writing to you.*

Cabaret! I have no idea what to expect. Have you ever been to a cabaret show? I wasn't sure how to dress for it either—when I asked Anna she just laughed and told me to use my imagination—so I'm wearing the red top you gave me, the button-down one with the sleeves that flare out and curl from the elbows. I can't believe I still have it—it's been, what, ten years, three moves? It's not fitting so great now—since I started taking derby more seriously (I'm EMILY THE SLAYER now! Strong like Buffy!), my arms have gotten huge, and you should see the butt on me— but it's still pretty and I love it, and it still matches my favourite earrings best.

I should probably tell you more about Anna, since obviously there's more to her than being trans and my co-worker. She's really great, and really *cute—she just cut her hair short last week and dyed it bright orange-red, so she looks kind of like Leeloo from* The Fifth Element. *She's vegan (sometimes I swear she likes the fact that I'm not, because it gives her an excuse to play "Meat is Murder" on loop in the cafe for the duration of my lunch break, which no one notices, because it sounds like every other Smiths song except the good ones, which she refuses to accept no matter how many times I explain it), an amazing cosplayer, and getting into burlesque. She hasn't performed in public yet, just for friends in her living room, but she's been developing this number that involves a chef's hat, mixed greens, and oversized serving implements.*

We're not dating or anything. I've only known her for about a month, though it feels like way longer—and I refuse to entertain a crush, because she's been in a closed poly triad for a while and they're kind of going through a rough patch that she hasn't told me much about. So I'll tell you more about this cabaret thing instead.

It's called SPANGLED CABARET ("spangled" is apparently one of about a million words that also means "wildly drunk" in the west of Scotland) and it happens once a month in this cafe, and Anna's been coming to it forever, basically. She really wants to perform here sometime once she feels confident enough.

It's also where she met her partners, Lynette and Kel. Kel's genderqueer and prefers "they" as a pronoun, so I'll try to keep this from getting confusing: they work nights at the airport, but Lynette's a performer, whose stage name is Lynette Byrd; her thing is apparently to dress up like a bird and sing?

Oh, she's just coming in. I'll write more later.

Love,
Emily

⌒

"Ooh, well done," said Anna, grinning, hooking her jacket over a chair. "These are the best seats in the house. Can I get you a drink?"

"The finest wines available to humanity," Emily declared, capping her pen and shutting the journal. She smiled up at her. "Something red?"

"Will do."

Emily watched her head to the bar. Anna, as usual, looked amazing, in a turquoise chiffon dress with ruffles at the neckline waving their way asymmetrically down the front, cinched at the waist with an orange belt that matched her hair.

She was also alone. When Anna returned with their drinks, Emily asked, "So, where's Lynette?"

"Oh, she can only hang out after her act. Something about 'diluting the effect'"—Anna made air quotes and rolled her eyes—"if she mingles with people beforehand. I hope that's okay—I thought we could have a little more time to talk before launching you into poly drama."

Emily chuckled. "That's fine. It's really cool to see you outside of work. You look awesome."

Anna grinned and tossed her short hair back dramatically. "Why thank you. So do you. That's a great blouse."

Emily blushed, looking down at her shirt. "Thanks, it was a gift—"

"It's very Romantic! Poet sleeves, fountain pen, leather-bound journal—excellent ensemble, though of course leather's murder too." Anna's smile was teasing. "It's beautiful, though. Where'd you find it?"

"Oh," she said, blushing hotter. "It was also a gift. From the same person. My best friend. The one I mentioned, Paige." She paused, uncertain how much more to say. "I write to her in it."

Anna blinked. "What?"

"You know, instead of letters. We each have one, and we write to each other in them whenever the mood takes us, and when they get full, or half-full, we post them to each other. We've been doing it for years—ever since she moved out west." She dropped it into her bag again, zipped it shut.

"That's so cool." Anna grinned. "You've actually found a way to make snail mail slower."

"Shut up! Not all of us want to have our phones embedded in our palms."

"Lies and trickery. You, too, lust for the Singularity in your heart of hearts."

"Those aren't even the same thing!"

The wine was good, the conversation easy. Emily felt herself relaxing, becoming aware of how little effort she was making, how unnecessary it felt to play at being wry and unaffected and vaguely disdainful of anything she passionately loved. By the time the lights dimmed and a tall man in red spats and cerulean trousers announced the beginning of the show, she was feeling excited.

The first act was a startling realization of Emily's earlier expectations, as a short bearded man unfolded a keyboard, flicked his coat-tails behind him, and sat down to play something melancholically sinister while a young woman in layers of fringed and shimmering fabric, loops of large white beads, and a flapper's red head scarf expertly drew a violin bow along the edge of a saw. The result was equal parts mournful and uncanny.

"That," shouted Emily over the subsequent applause, "was *amazing*. Is it all like this?"

Anna smiled. "Not quite."

The next act saw Emily covering her face while an attractive young man hammered nails up his nose.

"Come on," chuckled Anna, "it's not that bad! It's mostly tricks, anyway."

"Anna he's *bleeding*! He stuck a needle up his arm and *drew blood*."

"He's a professional!"

"His hands are shaking! This can't be right!"

"It's just part of the whole blockhead routine, honest. I've watched him do it loads of times."

"Really?" She dared a peek between her fingers, winced, and covered her eyes again.

"Really. Well. Not the needle, I think that's new, but the nails are standard. Oh, come on, you can't miss this, he's going to swallow those razors and knot them together in his throat—"

"*Hey*, I need the loo and we should have more drinks. Same again?"

"Sure, sure. Coward."

Emily stuck her tongue out and beat a hasty retreat.

It was equal parts the half-light, the show, and the wine, but the Rio had clearly slipped somewhere just slant of real. Navigating the distance between table and toilets felt like lucid dreaming. She passed men with moon-white faces in bowler hats; she washed her hands next to a woman in scarlet lingerie with mouse ears and a cheese-grater crotch. It felt like a secret carnival, like a place a runaway could call home.

She sat down again just as the blockhead was taking a bow, thankfully none the worse for wear. Anna looked positively fond as Emily pushed a new glass of wine toward her.

"You've got the look," Anna said, smiling.

"The look?"

"Of the hooked. The enchanted. You're one of us now."

"Just like that?" Emily looked dubious. "By running away from the blockhead?"

"It takes all sorts. I can't *wait* for you to see Lynette. She's usually on towards the end." Anna fiddled with a napkin. "She's . . . Something else. I could go on and on about her and not be able to say how."

"Are things . . ." Emily hesitated. "I mean, is it okay if I ask . . ."

Anna shrugged. "Things are things. The weirdness is mainly between Kel and me, but obviously Lynette's involved too, she can't not be. But—I can't really talk about it, sorry."

"That's totally fine. I don't want to pry! I just don't know what to expect, at all."

Anna chuckled. "That's probably for the best."

Once the applause died down, the emcee stepped forward to announce the final act, and encouraged everyone to stay precisely where they were.

Then the lights went out.

The cafe buzzed for a minute until a spotlight clicked on, shining up from the floor, illuminating a woman seated on a tall stool. But not completely—shadows striped her face and body, and as Emily took the scene in, she saw that the spotlight was shining through an ornate birdcage, projecting its bars against the wall and woman together.

When Anna said Lynette would be dressed as a bird, Emily had imagined something a bit camp, a bit silly, maybe a bit sexy into the bargain. She hadn't expected this tall, solemn, slender creature of angles and air, delicate golden-brown feathers sprouting from the shoulders, hips, and hem of a long white dress worn over slightly incongruous brown boots. Thick dark curls were piled on top of her head, against which leaned a high, feathered fascinator. There was an air of honey and copper about her, a shimmering sweetness. Emily's breath caught at the sight.

Lynette Byrd lifted her chin and regarded her audience coolly, head sharply tilted. When she parted her glittering lips and spoke, her voice was a sweep of warm light in the dim.

"Green finch and linnet bird! Nightingale! Blackbird!"

"*How is it you sing!*" shouted the audience members as one, making Emily jump a little in her seat. Lynette smiled.

"An oft-repeated question. Why does the caged bird sing? Why does it not embrace silence in protest, refusing to give up the thing for which it was imprisoned? Why, day after day, does it warble and sway from perch to perch, trilling its essence out in unrepeatable sequence for the benefit of its captors? *I am trusted,*" she laughed, suddenly, a sound like glass bursting, "*with a muzzle and enfranchised with a clog; therefore I have decreed not to sing in my cage.*"

With that she closed her eyes and leaned her cheek against the feathers on her shoulder, looking for all the world like a bird asleep.

Silence, then. Emily looked at Anna uncertainly, wondering if she should clap, but Anna was gazing at Lynette in rapt adoration. No one else seemed to think it was over, either. An uncomfortable minute passed, then two. A few people closed their eyes; a couple were staring intensely at their phones; one man nearby was moving his mouth without making a sound, and Emily realized he was counting. She turned back towards Lynette, who remained completely immobile. The sound of the bartender wiping crumbs from the counter became noticeable. She heard people shifting a little in their seats, though none spoke.

Emily frowned and looked down at her own phone. Had it been four minutes? Four minutes of—

Her eyes widened in sudden understanding. Before she knew what she was doing, she had gasped "OH!" out loud, to the shock of just about everyone else in the room.

She clapped her hands over her mouth in a panic, but Lynette didn't move—it was only every other head in the cafe that swung towards her, some frowning, some biting down a laugh, some laughing outright. She couldn't bring herself to look at Anna. Cheeks flushing, Emily fixed her eyes on the floor and tried to will it into melting away and taking her with it.

But only for another thirty seconds, as Lynette's performance of John Cage's *4'33"* came to an end. As people began to clap, Emily raised her head again.

Lynette had opened her eyes and was looking directly at her. She seemed amused.

"The reason, ultimately," she said, stretching her neck from one side to the other, and rolling back her feathered shoulders, "is that silence is terribly boring, no? Let us jubilate."

With that, Lynette launched into the most unearthly rendition of Sondheim's "Green Finch and Linnet Bird" Emily had ever heard. It was like sugar melting into caramel, hearing that bright, glittering song dimmed into a smoky minor key and twisted, stretched into so unlikely a shape. To listen was to feel her heart dragged over burrs, each turn of lyric snagging and pulling at her. By the time Lynette was asking the birds to teach her to be more adaptive, Emily had a pain in her throat and wet cheeks. Anna was quietly sobbing next to her.

Emily stretched out her hand without a word. Anna took it and squeezed.

It was like nothing else. She broke us open and read our entrails, I swear. It was like her art was a kind of sewing, a stitching together of things you'd never have thought could go together seamlessly. Hah. I just noticed how Seamstress is like a portmanteau of Seam and Mistress. Seam. Seem. Mistress of Seams and Seemings. I'm pretty drunk right now by the way.

So she's a Seemstress. She ended the show with a flick of her wrist, throwing a black cloth over the birdcage, and the spotlight clicked off. She didn't take a bow. She's drinking with Anna, now, they're talking, and I'm hiding in the bathroom because I can't bring myself to look at her even though I really want to talk to her and tell her how amazing it was. She came towards us after, and she looked at me in this way and said, "I truly enjoyed your contribution," and I just clammed up. I was so mortified. I don't think she even meant it to be mocking but I couldn't bear it. So I just sat there and got redder and redder and Anna took her attention off me, which is fine but I just felt like I'd failed, made the worst impression, and I just really needed to tell you about this right away, while it's all still hurting, the good and the bad of it, all together. I needed to tell you. I always need to tell you and you're not—you're never—

I wish—I wish you could have been here. Everything would be better if you were. I wish we could be talking about it right now. I wish—God, Paige, I miss you so fucking much. I miss you.

The ceiling came into focus first, and it was wrong: much too high, and the familiar pale orange stain that usually greeted her when she woke wasn't there. Then the smells: unfamiliar laundry detergent mixing with coffee like her father had it, with cardamom. The sound of water running, one wall over. Suddenly she bolted upright and took stock of the strange room, the strange bed, and the dull orange light coming through unfamiliar window slats from a street lamp outside. Still night-time, then.

She felt sick. Still drunk, obviously; the room kept threatening to spin, and her vision was anchored to a slow, awful churning in her belly. Was this Anna's place? Blearily, she swung her legs out of bed, and saw that she was still dressed. Quietly, she padded her way out of the room and into a dark hallway, towards the sound of water. She was thirsty. Her mouth felt full of sour cotton.

Light slanted into the hall from the half-open door to what she thought must be the bathroom; maybe Anna was brushing her teeth? She pushed it the rest of the way.

Lynette Byrd stood on one foot, lifting the hem of a white nightgown, one knee delicately raised above a bathtub filling with water. But her feet—Emily stared, blinked, shook her head, couldn't stop staring.

From the ankle down, Lynette's feet were the leathery, taloned, four-toed feet of a bird.

Lynette's eyes met hers, and she tilted her head as she had in her performance, but it had the look of a raptor now. Emily staggered back, watching Lynette's upraised knee lift higher, those talons flexing, swivelling away from the tub and onto the floor, clicking.

"Seemstress," she gasped, and the room spun faster and faster until she tumbled backwards into the dark.

When Emily woke again, it was to morning light filtering through the blankets over her head and whispering voices in the hall. She ventured a peek over the sheets, and saw Anna and Lynette in animated conversation, while someone who shared Lynette's height, cheekbones, and colouring stood silently by with arms folded. Kel? They had short-cropped black hair, sharp cheekbones, and human feet.

Lynette's remained disconcertingly taloned. She hadn't imagined it.

Emily rolled over and burrowed deeper into the blankets in search of oblivion.

"Hey," came Anna's voice, gently, from beyond the duvet. "Morning. How are you feeling?"

Emily tried to part her lips to say something intelligent and managed a tiny croak of misery. Anna patted her shoulder.

"Have some water. Come on, we won't bite. What do you remember?"

Slowly, Emily sat up, taking in the company. Anna, in pink flannel pajamas, looked concerned. Lynette without her make-up and feathers was still devastatingly beautiful: her black hair was a long sideways braid over her shoulder, and her light brown cheeks still had a hint of glitter to them. Her eyes were as black as her hair. She looked less like a magical bird-woman and more like someone from Emily's own family now—as did Kel, who was looking at Emily with distrust.

She accepted a glass of water and took small, careful sips. "Lynette has bird feet."

Anna winced. Kel muttered something under their breath that sounded like it was probably rude. Lynette waved her hand.

"We will speak of that later. I think Anna meant from earlier in the evening."

"Oh." She hadn't given it much thought. "I remember—sitting with you both, and then going to the bathroom, and, um." The shame of it, locking herself in a stall and crying, washed over her in a nauseous wave. "I guess Anna came in to check on me after a while. I don't remember much else."

"You seemed very upset." Lynette looked at her curiously. "I was concerned that I had said something to hurt you. Then you fell asleep, and Anna didn't know where you lived, so we brought you here instead."

Emily bit her lip, stared into her glass. "I'm so, so sorry—"

"It's no trouble, truly," said Lynette. Kel snorted at that, and Anna smacked them on the arm and glared. Lynette ignored them, focused on Emily. "*Did* I hurt you in some way?"

"No, I'm—I was just so embarrassed. About the John Cage thing. Everything had been going so well until that point, and now I've fucked everything up, and you—you're being so *nice*—"

"Emily." Anna looked pained. "You haven't done anything wrong."

Emily looked at her, and felt something tightly wound in her release. She felt suddenly ragged with relief.

"Really? You're not angry?"

"Angry?" Anna stared at her. "Emily, you just found out my girlfriend's part bird and you're worried about what *I* think?"

"I think," said Lynette, "that we should have some coffee. Would you like that, Emily?"

"Yes, please." She looked at Kel uncertainly. "Are you—are you going to curse me or erase my memory or something?"

Lynette blinked. So did Anna and Kel. All three of them looked at each other. To Emily's discomfort, they all burst out laughing.

"That," said Lynette, "would be terrible manners."

"That's—not a 'no,' though." Emily had the feeling of being in a dream, of watching herself having this conversation. Lynette only smiled, looking as if she was enjoying herself.

"Emily, if you'll forgive me the presumption, what is your surname?"

"Haddad."

"Then we both hail from places where hospitality is sacrosanct, and one would not offer coffee to a guest to whom one intended any harm. Come. Let us have a sobhiyeh."

The coffee tasted of home, of dawns spent with her father in comfort and certainty and safety. Kel remained quiet, and Anna's focus was on them more than Emily, but Lynette was shockingly easy to talk to. Emily found herself pouring out the history of her last year: the master's degree in library sciences in London, how unbearable she'd found life in the city, how brutal the sarcasm that passed for affection, how she only hated herself more for not being able to banter with her colleagues and their friends, how she never felt entirely welcome among them.

"It's like everything I took for granted about friendship, and language, about what's polite and what isn't—it's not a default. We're taught—I was taught—that it's somehow universal, to be kind and open and welcoming and sincere, and it's not. And worse, it's not that it's *bad* not to be that way, there. There, it makes sense, how closed off and distant and biting everyone is. It's just a different way of being, that's all. But it's hard not to feel like everything about me is *wrong*—the way I laugh, the things I laugh at or don't. My words, my accent, the things I think are cruel. It's like, to live there, I needed to . . . tailor myself. Cut off bits that don't fit, or stuff them away, and sometimes I'd look in a mirror and just not recognize myself for the silence."

Kel stood up, abruptly.

"I'm going to bed," they said, gruffly, in a low voice. "Sorry. Long night."

Emily faltered. "Okay."

"I'll join you," said Anna, getting up. "Just for a bit."

Kel muttered something by way of assent. Anna looked apologetically at Emily before following Kel and shutting the door behind them.

"So," said Lynette, sipping her coffee from a tiny porcelain cup, turning her attention back to Emily. "Where were we. You finished your degree, yes? Why not go home to Canada? Why come to Glasgow instead?"

"Oh—" she sighed, swirled her coffee around her cup, watched the patterns the grains made against it. "I love my family, and I miss them. A lot. But—I'm queer, and they're not okay with that. I mean," she rushed to say, "they're not horrible or anything. We've had the 'we'll still love you no matter what' talk and whatever. But I just—I never really dated anyone when I was home. At all. And suddenly here, awful as everything else got, I went on dates, I flirted with men and women, and—part of me is more *me* here, I guess. I'm not done with that yet."

"Even though everything else feels wrong?"

Emily chuckled, not without bitterness. "Yeah. I'm crying you a river, I know." She finished the rest of her coffee in a gulp. Lynette leaned forward and poured more.

"It's the plight of the displaced, Emily. The stuff of song and story. People here are fond of saying that all the most loving songs about Scotland are written by those who left." Lynette replenished her own cup, and lifted it contemplatively. "One leaves home, one misses it; one makes a home as best one can, with the materials at hand, knowing it will never be what one had; but there are reasons, always good reasons, why one left in the first place." Before Emily could ask anything, Lynette smiled. "But, Glasgow? Why not stay in London?"

"Honestly?" She smiled a little. "I'd never been to Scotland yet, and I loved the names of Glasgow's derby teams. Irn Bruisers? Maiden Grrders? Seemed like reason enough."

Lynette laughed, and Emily found herself thinking of flowers. She took another sip of her coffee, and waited.

"Well," said Lynette, a touch of amusement still there, "I suppose it's my turn. Do you know what a Peri is?"

Emily blinked, brain flashing through Patricia McKillip, *Doctor Who*, and hot sauce. "Er—"

Lynette smiled. "That's quite all right. Whatever you do, don't read the Wikipedia entry. Nineteenth-century Englishmen with their books and operas did more to secure ignorance about us than the Severing of Seventy Bridges. Suffice to say we are a kind of—what you would call spirit. We are not human, though we sometimes enjoy human form. We have a world, our own world, that overlaps and intersects with yours"—here Lynette clasped her hands together, fingers interweaving—"and in which we are ourselves. But without access to it"—Lynette fixed her gaze on somewhere just over Emily's shoulder, as if the world she spoke of was just there—"we are less. We lose our ability to shift our shapes, to fly, to be flame or water. We become solid, locked. We"—she drew her gaze back to Emily—"cut off bits that don't fit, or stuff them away, and sometimes we look in a mirror and can't recognize ourselves. We are wrong. We are *less*." Lynette paused to sip her coffee, and licked her lips thoughtfully. "Though we are also sometimes more."

Emily felt a lump rising in her throat. "How?"

Lynette lost, for a moment, the air of knowing amusement she'd worn for most of their acquaintance, and looked only wistful. "I was no performer, back home. I had no art. It was here, in this place, that I found my voice." When she smiled again, it was soft, and pained. "I did not learn to sing until I was shut in a cage."

Emily frowned. "Shut? But—didn't you leave on purpose?"

She shrugged. "To the extent that being forced to flee is 'on purpose.' Kel and I—"

"Wait, Kel's a Peri too?" Emily stared. "But—Kel's feet—"

Lynette chuckled. "We all have different tells. Were Kel to show you their back, you would see two lines of black feathers angled along their spine. May I continue?"

She flushed. "Please."

"We were . . . 'Exiled' is perhaps not the right word. Our country is at war, Emily. We are, in a sense, refugees. We fled, and the door shut behind us. Kel wants nothing so much as to go back, to fight, to die, if necessary. I do not. As much as I long for wings again—" Lynette's voice caught, and she looked down, and shook her head slowly. "No. For better or for worse, I am making a life here." She chuckled. "Though it is difficult not to laugh, or weep, when someone asks me where I am 'from.'"

"I sort of know what *that*'s like," Emily murmured. "'Where are you from?' 'Canada.' 'Yeah, yeah, where are your PARENTS from.'" Emily mimed throttling an invisible neck, and Lynette chuckled. "It's not as bad here, actually. Mostly people assume I'm American." She paused, thoughtful. "So—why doesn't Kel go back?"

"Ah." Lynette put down her cup, folded her hands in her lap. "They cannot afford the cost."

"The cost?"

"Indeed. Our world is the source of our power; when the way is open, we can shift our shapes, fly, find things that are hidden or missing, carry our lovers across the world in our arms if we so choose. When the way is shut"—Lynette shrugged—"there is a cost to open it. At present it is as if Kel and I have been stripped of citizenship, and must apply for visas instead of coming and going as we please. And, as with visas, there is always the chance that after having paid the price and sent in our paperwork, our application will be rejected all the same. . . . Are you all right?"

Emily nodded, tight-lipped. "Sorry, I just—what do you mean, find things that are hidden or missing?"

"It's just an ability we possess." Lynette looked at her curiously. "A function of our nature."

"Oh." She nodded again. "Please go on. What *is* the cost?"

Lynette considered her for a moment longer before answering. "It is . . . an elaboration of the usual shedding of a form. For us, to open the way, we must give up a whole person. A sacrifice, if you will."

Emily stared at her. "What, you mean—you have to *kill* someone?"

Lynette shook her head. "Not kill. Give up. Relinquish. But it only works if the person is precious, beloved. For me—if I were to cut out my tongue, I might be able to open the way back. I would be giving up who I have become here, my art. Once on the other side I might easily choose a different form, one with a tongue, perhaps one with a more beautiful voice—but I would lose Lynette Byrd, whom I have come to love, and I would never have her again. That is *if* the sacrifice is deemed sufficient."

"So, Kel—"

"Kel loves nothing about who they are here. Every moment spent in their body is torment. Kel never kept one body for long, understand—if you comprehend gender on a spectrum of male and female, think of us as possessing gender along a spectrum of fluid and fixed. It is agony for Kel to be in one body, to be static, to be observable always in the same way." Lynette sighed. "It is an exquisitely devised exile. We must love something so much that we could never wish to give it up—and then give it up. So long as Kel despises their body, they cannot shed it, and so long as they cannot shed it, they will always despise their body and the world it is forced to inhabit. The only things they have come to love, while here, are the River Kelvin, from which they take their name—and Anna. But not enough. Kel is too willing to give them up. I had hoped that perhaps with Anna—with someone who understood the pain of a body that feels wrong—" Lynette shook her head. "As soon as Kel began to feel deeper affection for her, they sought to barter it for passage."

Emily blinked. "Kel tried to give Anna up?"

"Yes." Lynette looked pained. "There is a ritual we do, by the river, to open the way home. Anna participated, willingly—but it wasn't enough. The trap works too well. Kel might have once loved me enough for the leaving to hurt sufficiently, but—" She closed her eyes, briefly. "It is hard for them, that I will not give up myself to pay for the chance of our passage. And so it goes. The magic must be cruel, to work. It must feel like the tearing of a page."

Emily felt a sudden pang—a tug in her belly, like cresting the topmost hill of a roller coaster, teetering on the edge of the plunge.

"So, without your powers, you can't open the way back, and until that way is open, you don't have your powers?"

Lynette opened her eyes again, and nodded. Emily bit her lip.

"And could—anyone open up the way? By giving something up?"

"In theory." Emily felt her cheeks flushing beneath the sudden intensity of Lynette's gaze. "What are you saying?"

"I'm saying—suppose someone wanted you to have your powers. For something specific. Would you—could you help them, if the door was open?"

Lynette said nothing for a long moment, while Emily met her eyes. When Lynette finally spoke, it was gentle.

"What have you lost, Emily?"

She pulled her backpack onto her lap, unzipped it, pulled out her journal, and put it on the table between them.

"My best friend."

◦∼

Dear Paige,

I told Lynette about you. It was hard, at first. For so long you've felt like a secret I've been keeping on your behalf. My best friend, to whom I write—who never writes back. My best friend, whom I've known for half my life—but who hasn't spoken to me in over a year. My best friend, who was going to travel with me, share a home with me, be up against the world with me—who vanished into air and darkness and didn't tell me where she was going.

It was hard, but it got easier.

I told her how afraid I've become for you. I told her about your depression, how you'd been withdrawing for a while, that it got worse once we had extra time zones between us. I told her about the unanswered phone messages, e-mails, postcards. I told her about how I called your work one time just to see if they could tell me you were alive, and how they said they'd laid you off a week earlier, and didn't know how to answer my question about whether or not you were okay.

She asked me if I was prepared to find out that you're dead. I told her that I knew you couldn't be dead, couldn't possibly be, because I'd know. I'd feel something snap. I'm sure I would.

She told me to prepare for the possibility all the same.

So this is the last I'm writing to you in here. I'm giving you up—sort of—to find you. It may not work. It may not be enough. But I told Lynette that I'm giving up years of myself in here, too— the me who is best friends with Paige, who is happy and secure and confident, who can see friendships come and go because at her core is this one, this unshakeable soul-twin sister-friend who'll never leave her.

So long as I've been writing in here I've felt like I could still be that person, because by writing to you I am conjuring you, I am keeping you in existence, and if you exist, so do I. And maybe if I find you—if Lynette can find you—she said Peri magics include carrying people through the air, so—if you're in trouble, if you're hurt—I can't even think about that but I have to trust in something, that this will be okay, somehow. That I can still be some kind of me even without you.

I love you. I'm giving you up.
Emily

⌒

Lynette and Kel had gone ahead, saying they had preparations to make. Anna watched as Emily laced her boots in the entrance to their flat. "I can't believe you're doing this. *Why* would you do this. You hardly even know them."

Emily shrugged. "It's not for them. It's for Paige. And—for me."

"Bullshit."

Emily flinched and looked up, hurt. "What possible other reason could I have?"

Anna folded her arms, looked away. "Whatever, I don't care."

"Do you not want me to do this?"

Anna rolled her eyes. "Think about it for two seconds, Emily."

"But Lynette said you wanted—"

"*Fuck* Lynette." Anna brushed a lock of hair behind her ear. "Look, I just—I love Kel. I fucking love them. And it's—hard, to make peace with losing someone for their own good, to know that you're the price of their happiness, and to agree to pay that price and then have it not be enough, because actually they didn't love you enough, you know?" She exhaled, pushed the heel of her palm into her eye. "And here you are, having only just met them, making some kind of huge weird sacrifice, and if it works—" Anna choked. "If it works, then I lose Kel, and nothing about it was noble, nothing about it was *my* sacrifice. I'm just another failed attempt to get home."

"That's not true," said Emily, shocked, standing up so quickly she stumbled. "Anna—"

"Shut up. Go to the river, do whatever needs doing. I get it. Been there, done that." They looked at each other through tears. "I hope you find your friend."

Then Anna walked into her bedroom and slammed the door behind her. Emily tried not to cry as she let herself out.

⸻

They stood together by the river's edge beneath the bridge on Gibson Street. Emily clutched her journal to her chest and shivered as Kel waded into the water barefoot. As they did, the river seemed somehow to swell up around them, grow deeper than it was; once it reached their lips, Kel stopped.

Emily could hear Kel murmuring something into the water. Lynette stood next to her, wearing her cabaret costume and clutching a fistful of flower petals. She spoke quietly.

"You know what you need to do?"

Emily nodded.

"Very well. Kel is almost finished asking the river's permission to pass through." She looked away. "I hope this works. I don't know how Kel will bear it otherwise."

Emily swallowed, thinking of Anna. "I hope it works too."

Kel stopped speaking, and began undressing in the water. As they removed their shirt, Emily saw the two long black lines of feathers running to either side of Kel's spine like sutures, glinting in the dim light.

Kel turned to look at them, and nodded once. Lynette closed her eyes.

"It's time."

She drew a deep breath, cast the petals into the water, and began singing Arcade Fire's "My Body Is a Cage." While she did, Emily took a few steps into the water and opened the journal. She looked down and couldn't help but read a line—from an early entry, a happy day, speaking of how exciting it was to be in England, how she'd been to the Sir John Soane's Museum and tried to count all the busts for science.

As she grasped the page and pulled, she couldn't tell if it was she or the paper who was tearing.

Then she staggered. The world tilted, and she felt herself struggling to hold her breath.

Something was happening to the water—a churning where it had been still, a circling of light flooding upwards around Kel. Emily tore another page, and another, throwing each one into the river, sobs welling up as she did, cutting into her throat every time she read, in spite of herself, a snippet of something Paige would never read, never know—her conviction that a different sun shone over London, made of syrup and smoke; the dream she had on Halloween after her first gin and tonic; her first kiss with a woman. She'd meant to share it all with Paige, show her this new person she was becoming, and if Paige never saw her, was any of her real?

Lynette was still singing—*set my spirit free, set my body free*—but she sounded farther and farther away. Emily could see the light around Kel brightening, and Kel—Kel was changing. The twin lines of feathers on their back were growing out, covering more and more skin, and Kel's body was blurring in and out of the water. Could it be working? Was it enough, after all? Would she find—

Lynette's song ended. Half a beat after the final note, Emily heard her say, as if she were shouting from a vast distance away, *look into the water.*

She looked. In the same brightness she had seen shimmering around Kel, there was Paige.

The sight sank into her like a knife. There was Paige, in a laundromat—she was seeing her from behind, her long pale hair twisted up into a bun. She was taking washing out of one machine and putting it in a dryer. She was humming something, happily.

Overwhelmingly, Emily knew she was happy.

I can bring her to you, thundered Lynette's voice, *if you wish. In half a moment or less.*

She did wish. She wanted, so badly, to have her in front of her, to rage and scream *how, how could you be happy and all right and not speak to me, why wouldn't you, what did I do wrong, what.*

Paige was happy, washing laundry, and had her back to her. Emily stretched her hand into the water, choking on everything she wanted to say. But she'd said it already, into the river, as Anna had said it to Kel.

She drew her hand back.

"No," she whispered. "She's fine where she is."

Then the light dimmed, the river smoothed, and Emily found herself weeping into the down on Lynette's shoulder.

༄

Dear Emily,

This is probably cheating, but you never specified the size of journal required, and a palm-sized Moleskine is still a Moleskine, and that means journal, so. Here I am, writing to you in a journal. My penmanship peaked in Primary 6. I hope you're happy.

I'm sorry for—well, everything. I hope I didn't hurt you too badly by keeping away for a while—that's why I'm writing in here, for now. I figured maybe we both needed a little space after what happened. But—well, I miss you. I miss talking to you. This is a piss-poor substitute, actually. But I guess it's better than nothing, and I think you might like, maybe, to know that I pay attention to the things you say even if I also tease you about them a little.

So I don't know how long I'll keep this up—it's a small book, and it's not meant to replace anything, obviously. It couldn't. I don't know how you'll feel about it when I give it to you. I just want you to know, basically, that I still really like you, that I think you're grand, that I'm grateful you're not a jerk, and maybe if you're up for it we could go to Nice N'Sleazy's sometime for a gig? I think you'd like it, the ceiling lights are covered in paper shades with clubs, spades, hearts, and diamonds on them.

Oh, you're just coming in for your shift. I'll write more later.

Love,
Anna

THUNDERSTORM IN GLASGOW, JULY 25, 2013

Rattle my heart, four-chambered sound
loosen my language from my teeth
tumble *raaed* out from a fallow throat
and a forgotten year

when hunched in barracks beneath the rain
that gushed from gutters, corrugated roofs
one sister clutched her mother's hand
and one strained, strained against her grip
wanting the wet, the loud, the dark, the bright,
to shake hands with that searing flash
and make it her friend.

Say *aasfi*, say *ghaymi*,
unbury the words with this digging rain,
remember how gardens seemed to sprout from stone
as water struck it, drops unnumbered
fountaining upwards as if to try
for a place in the sky again.

Say *aaskar*, say *hammam*,
recall wondering why soldiers
needed such a big bathroom anyway—
while the storm sluiced over eaves and doors
and stirred into the sea—

gather the words like clouds to burst,
but remember too, the vicious truth:
when the sky lashed hard and cracked the air,
when you hipped your fists and stared it down,

shouting patience, shouting peace
as only a child can—

you left *raaed, ghaymi, aasfi, hammam,
aaskar* in your mother's hand,
spoke English to the rain.

ANABASIS

A warning is the same as a threat. Television teaches this. *Is that a threat / Call it a warning.* Call it by a different name, and it changes.

Snow is only slow, cold rain. Only rain.

Her child said, *Mama, I want to die in the snow.*

I am a shape-shifter. Most people are. We change our shapes day on day, replace cells, grow muscles and fat, shed hair, grow it back lighter, darker. Some of us do it faster, is all—some of us have specialties.

My specialty is mouths.

My real mouth is full of sharp teeth and a sharper tongue, three languages coiled like snakes in my throat, scaly and silent. My real mouth is an armoury of words forged in the furnace of my chest, hot as a spitted sun. My real mouth is a storm, and my voice is thunder.

To pass among you I wear a different mouth: full lips unparted, always smiling. I paint it pretty colours. It speaks only when spoken to, softly. To pass among you, it tells you stories:

I am sweetness. I am sunshine. I am here to hold your hand through the horror of my name.

My mouth is a coin, and I spend it.

An explanation is the same as an excuse. There are agreements, laws, protocols; there are pieces of paper more important than her child's pain.

She was given an explanation as if it were a blanket, or food, or shelter. She was given an explanation as if it were a gift, to be purchased with gratitude.

She walked past it, into the snow.

⁓

Borders are shape-shifters, too: they change what goes through them. Time was, the only border worth crossing was into the underworld, to fetch back a lover's life: *Take off your shoes*, said Ereshkigal to Inanna, *your belt, your rings. Take off your armour, your hair, your skin, your flesh. Set your bones aside separately; bag your liquids. Do you have any sensitive areas—*

We cross into the sky now. *Plus ça change.*

My passport is a blue rectangle stamped *Canada*. My name is inside it. The border's eye falls on it and shifts it into *threat*. The border's eye looks at me and we wrestle, as his eye tries to change me into *Arab* or *Muslim*, and I struggle to remain *Canadian*.

My mouth does most of the work. My mouth is soft and yielding; my mouth is what books call *generous*. My mouth does not get angry. My mouth spills its English out as tribute, smooth seamless scales gleaming in the fluorescent light.

⁓

The cold has a mouth. It eats fingers and toes, nibbles ears like a paperback lover. She knew the stories of bodies carved into classical sculpture, here missing a hand, there a foot, a nose. She knew the border is a wire that shears bodies into meat, to be chewed and spat out again, one bloody gobbet at a time. She knew it.

The only mouth that matters is her child's, gnawing her heart one word at a time.

So she walks.

⁓

If I could take each of my words and lay them in the snow at her feet. If I could take each of my mouths and eat this distance between us. If I could devour this border, if I could tell it to smile while I broke its teeth, if I could unsheathe the sword of my mouth and strike it down, if I could thread the needle of my mouth and stitch good shoes for her baby, if I could cut a path into this country with the sharpness of my tongue—

If I could change the world as easily as my mouth . . .

With the whole of my furnace-heart, I would. But I can't.

Instead I follow her footsteps as if they could lead me outside myself, into a country we already share.

TO FOLLOW THE WAVES

Hessa's legs ached. She knew she ought to stand, stretch them, but only gritted her teeth and glared at the clear lump of quartz on the table before her. To rise now would be to concede defeat—but to lean back, lift her goggles, and rub her eyes was, she reasoned, an adequate compromise.

Her braids weighed on her, and she scratched the back of her head, where they pulled tightest above her nape. To receive a commission from Sitt Warda Al-Attrash was a great honour, one that would secure her reputation as a fixed star among Dimashq's dream-crafters. She could not afford to fail. Worse, the dream Sitt Warda desired was simple, as dreams went: to be a young woman again, bathing her limbs by moonlight in the Mediterranean with a young man who, judging by her half-spoken, half-murmured description, was not precisely her husband.

But Hessa had never been to the sea.

She had heard it spoken of, naturally, and read hundreds of lines of poetry extolling its many virtues. Yet it held little wonder for her; what pleasure could be found in stinging salt, scratching sand, burning sun reflected from the water's mirror-surface? Nor did swimming hold any appeal; she had heard pearl divers boast of their exploits, speak of how the blood beat between their eyes until they felt their heads might burst like overripe tomatoes, how their lungs ached with the effort for hours afterward, how sometimes they would feel as if thousands of ants were marching along their skin, and though they scratched until blood bloomed beneath their fingernails, could never reach them.

None of this did anything to endear the idea of the sea to her. And yet, to carve the dream out of the quartz, she had to find its beauty. Sighing, she picked up the dop stick, tapped the quartz to make sure it was securely fastened, lowered her goggles, and tried again.

Hessa's mother was a mathematician, renowned well beyond the gates of Dimashq for her theorems. Her father was a poet, better known for his abilities as an artisanal cook than for his verse, though as the latter was full of the scents and flavours of the former, much appreciated all the same. Hessa's father taught her to contemplate what was pleasing to the senses, while her mother taught her geometry and algebra. She loved both as she loved them, with her whole heart.

Salma Najjar had knocked at the door of the Ghaflan family in the spring of Hessa's seventh year. She was a small woman, wrinkled as a wasp's nest, with eyes hard and bright as chips of tourmaline. Her greying hair was knotted and bound in the intricate patterns of a jeweller or gem-cutter—perhaps some combination of the two. Hessa's parents welcomed her into their home, led her to a divan, and offered her tea, but she refused to drink or eat until she had told them her errand.

"I need a child of numbers and letters to learn my trade," she had said, in the gruff, clipped accent of the Northern cities. "It is a good trade, one that will demand the use of all her abilities. I have heard that your daughter is such a child."

"And what is your trade?" Hessa's father asked, intrigued, but wary.

"To sculpt fantasies in the stone of the mind and the mind of the stone. To grant wishes."

"You propose to raise our daughter as djinn?" Hessa's mother raised an eyebrow.

Salma smiled, showing a row of perfect teeth. "Far better. Djinn do not get paid."

Building a dream was as complex as building a temple, and required knowledge of almost as many trades—a fact reflected in the complexity of the braid pattern in which Hessa wore her hair. Each pull and plait showed an intersection of gem-crafting, metal-working, architecture, and storytelling, to say nothing of the thousand twisting strands representing the many kinds of knowledge necessary to a story's success. As a child, Hessa had spent hours with the archivists in Al-Zahiriyya Library, learning from them the art of constructing memory palaces within her mind, layering the marble, glass, and mosaics of her imagination with reams of poetry, important historical dates, dozens of musical maqaamat, names of stars and ancestors. *Hessa bint Aliyah bint Qamar bint Widad*...

She learned to carry each name, note, number like a jewel to tuck into a drawer here, hang above a mirror there, for ease of finding later on. She knew whole geographies, scriptures, story cycles, as intimately as she knew her mother's house, and drew on them whenever she received a commission. Though the only saleable part of her craft was the device she built with her hands, its true value lay in using the materials of her mind: She could not grind quartz to the shape and tune of her dream, could not set it into the copper coronet studded with amber, until she had fixed it into her thoughts as firmly as she fixed the stone to her amber dop stick.

"Every stone," Salma said, tossing her a piece of rough quartz, "knows how to sing. Can you hear it?"

Frowning, Hessa held it up to her ear, but Salma laughed. "No, no. It is not a shell from the sea, singing the absence of its creature. You cannot hear the stone's song with the ear alone. Look at it; feel it under your hand; you must learn its song, its language, before you can teach it your own. You must learn, too, to tell the stones apart; those that sing loudest do not always have the best memories, and it is memory that is most important. Easier to teach it to sing one song beautifully than to teach it to remember; some stones can sing nothing but their own tunes."

Dream-crafting was still a new art then; Salma was among its pioneers. But she knew that she did not have within herself what it would take to excel at it. Having discovered a new instrument, she found it unsuited to her fingers, awkward to rest against her heart; she could produce sound, but not music.

For that, she had to teach others to play.

First, she taught Hessa to cut gems. That had been Salma's own trade, and Hessa could see that it was still her chief love: the way she smiled as she turned a piece of rough crystal in her hands, learning its angles and texture, was very much the way Hessa's parents smiled at each other. She taught her how to pick the best stones, cleave away their grossest imperfections; she taught her to attach the gem to a dop stick with hot wax, at precise angles, taught her the delicate dance of holding it against a grinding lathe with even greater precision while operating the pedal. She taught her to calculate the axes that would unlock needles of light from the stone, kindle fire in its heart. Only once Hessa could grind a cabochon blindfolded, once she'd learned to see with the tips of her fingers, did Salma explain the rest.

"This is how you will teach songs to the stone." She held up a delicate amber wand, at the end of which was affixed a small copper vice. Hessa watched as Salma placed a cloudy piece of quartz inside and adjusted the vice around it before lowering her goggles over her eyes. "The amber catches your thoughts and speaks them to the copper; the copper translates them to the quartz. But just as you build your memory palace in your mind, so must you build the dream you want to teach it; first in your thoughts, then in the stone. You must cut the quartz while fixing the dream firmly in your mind, that you may cut the dream into the stone, cut it so that the dream blooms from it like light. Then, you must fix it into copper and amber again, that the dream may be translated into the mind of the dreamer.

"Tonight," she murmured quietly, grinding edges into the stone, "you will dream of horses. You will stand by a river and they will run past you, but one will slow to a stop. It will approach you, and nuzzle your cheek."

"What colour will it be?"

Salma blinked behind her goggles, and the lathe slowed to a stop as she looked at her. "What colour would you like it to be?"

"Blue," said Hessa, firmly. It was her favourite colour.

Salma frowned. "There are no blue horses, child."

"But this is a dream! Couldn't I see one in a dream?"

Hessa wasn't sure why Salma was looking at her with quite such intensity, or why it took her so long a moment to answer. But finally, she smiled—in the gentle, quiet way she smiled at her gems—and said, "Yes, my heart. You could."

Once the quartz was cut, Salma fixed it into the centre of a copper circlet, its length prettily decorated with drops of amber, and fitted it around Hessa's head before giving her chamomile tea to drink and sending her to bed. Hessa dreamed just as Salma said she would: The horse that approached her was blue as the turquoise she had shaped for a potter's husband a few nights earlier. But when the horse touched her, its nose was dry and cold as quartz, its cheeks hard and smooth as cabochon.

Salma sighed when Hessa told her as much the next day. "You see, this is why I teach you, Hessa. I have been so long in the country of stones, speaking their language and learning their songs, I have little to teach them of our own; I speak everything to them in facets and brilliance, culets and crowns. But you, my dear, you are learning many languages at once; you have your father's tasting tongue, your mother's speech of angles and air. I have been speaking nothing but adamant for most of my life, and grow more and more deaf to the desires of dreamers."

⁓

Try as she might, Hessa could not coordinate her knowledge of the sea with the love, the longing, the pleasure needed to build Sitt Warda's dream. She had mixed salt and water, touched it to her lips, and found it unpleasant; she had watched the moon tremble in the waters of her courtyard's fountain without being able to stitch its beauty to a horizon. She tried, now, to summon those poor attempts to mind, but was keenly aware that if she began grinding the quartz in her present state, Sitt Warda would wake from her dream as tired and frustrated as she herself presently felt.

Giving in, she put down the quartz, removed her goggles, rose from her seat, and turned her back on her workshop. There were some problems only coffee and ice cream could fix.

Qahwat al Adraj was one of her favourite places to sit and do the opposite of think. Outside the bustle of the Hamadiyyah market, too small and plain to be patronised by obnoxious tourists, it was a well-kept secret tucked beneath a dusty stone staircase: The servers were attentive, the coffee exquisite, and the iced treats in summer particularly fine. As she closed the short distance between it and her workshop, she tried to force her gaze up from the dusty path her feet had long ago memorised, tried to empty herself of the day's frustrations to make room for her city's beauties.

There: a young man with dark skin and a dazzling smile, his tight-knotted braids declaring him a merchant-inventor, addressing a gathering crowd to display his newest brass automata. "Ladies and gentlemen," he called, "the English Chef!" and demonstrated how with a few cranks and a minimum of preparation, the long-faced machine could knife carrots into twisting orange garlands, slice cucumbers into lace. And not far from him, drawn to the promise of a building audience, a beautiful mechanical, her head sculpted to look like an amira's headdress, serving coffee from the heated cone of it by tipping forward in an elegant bow before the cup, an act that could not help but make every customer feel as if they were sipping the gift of a cardamom-laced dance.

Hessa smiled to them, but frowned to herself. She had seen them all many times before. Today she was conscious, to her shame, of a bitterness toward them: What business had they being beautiful to her when they were not the sea?

Arriving, she took her usual seat by a window that looked out to Touma's Gate, sipped her own coffee, and tried not to brood.

She knew what Salma would have said. *Go to the sea*, she would have urged, *bathe in it! Or, if you cannot, read the thousands of poems written to it! Write a poem yourself! Or,* slyly, then, *only think of something you yourself find beautiful—horses, berries, books—and hide it beneath layers and layers of desire until the thing you love is itself obscured. Every pearl has a grain of sand at its heart, no? Be cunning. You cannot know all the world, my dear, as intimately as you know your stones.*

But she couldn't. She had experimented with such dreams, crafted them for herself; they came out wrapped in cotton wool, provoking feeling without vision, touch, scent. Any would-be dream-crafter could do as well. No, for Sitt Warda, who had already patronised four of the city's crafters before her, it would never do. She had to produce something exquisite, unique. She had to know the sea as Sitt Warda knew it, as she wanted it.

She reached for a newspaper, seeking distraction. Lately it was all airships and trade agreements surrounding their construction and deployment, the merchant fleets' complaints and clamour for restrictions on allowable cargo to protect their own interests. Hessa had a moment of smirking at the sea-riding curmudgeons before realizing that she had succumbed, again, to the trap of her knotting thoughts. Perhaps if the sea were seen from a great height? But that would provoke the sensation of falling, and Sitt Warda did not want a flying dream . . .

Gritting her teeth, she buried her face in her hands—until she heard someone step through the doorway, sounding the hollow glass chimes in so doing. Hessa looked up.

A woman stood there, looking around, the early afternoon light casting a faint nimbus around her, shadowing her face. She was tall, and wore a long, simple dark blue coat over a white dress, its embroidery too plain to declare a regional origin. Hessa could see she had beautiful hands, the gold in them drawn out by the midnight of the blue, but it was not these at which she found herself staring. It was the woman's hair.

Unbound, it rippled.

There was shame in that, Hessa had always felt, had always been taught. To wear one's hair so free in public was to proclaim oneself unbound to a trade, useless; even the travellers who passed through the city bound knots into their hair out of respect for custom, the five braids of travellers and visitors who wished themselves known as such above anything else, needing hospitality or good directions. The strangeness of it thrilled and stung her.

It would perhaps not have been so shocking were it one long unbroken sheet of silk, a sleek spill of ink with no light in it. But it rippled, as if just released from many braids, as if fingers had already tangled there, as if hot breath had moistened it to curling waves. *Brazen*, thought Hessa, the word snagging on half-remembered lines of English poetry, *brazen greaves, burnish'd hooves.* Unfamiliar words, strange, like a spell—and suddenly it was a torrent of images, of rivers and aching and spilling and immensity, because she wanted that hair in her own hand, wanted to see her skin vanish into its blackness, wanted it to swallow her while she swallowed it—

It took her a moment to notice the woman was looking at her. It took another for Hessa to flush with the understanding that she was staring rudely before dropping her gaze back to her coffee. She counted to seventy in her head before daring to look up again: By the time she did, the woman was seated, a server half-hiding her from Hessa's view. Hessa laid money on the table and rose to leave, taking slow, deliberate steps toward the door. As soon as she was outside the coffee house, she broke into a run.

Two nights later, with a piece of finely shaped quartz pulsing against her brow, Sitt Warda Al-Attrash dreamed of her former lover with honeysuckle sweetness, and if the waves that rose and fell around them were black and soft as hair, she was too enraptured to notice.

Hessa could not stop thinking of the woman. She took to eating most of her meals at Qahwat al Adraj, hoping to see her again—to speak, apologise for what must have seemed appalling behaviour, buy her a drink—but the woman did not return. When she wasn't working, Hessa found her fingertips tracing delicate, undulating lines through the gem dust that coated her table, thighs tightly clenched, biting her lip with longing. Her work did not suffer for it—if anything, it improved tremendously. The need to craft flooded her, pushed her to pour the aching out into copper and crystal.

Meantime, Sitt Warda could not stop speaking of Hessa, glowing in her praise; she told all her wealthy friends of the gem among dream-crafters who dimmed all others to ash, insisting they sample her wares. Where before Hessa might have had one or two commissions a week, she began to receive a dozen a day, and found herself in a position to pick and choose among them. This she did—but it took several commissions before she saw what was guiding her choice.

"Craft me a dream of the ruins of Baalbek," said one kind-eyed gentleman with skin like star-struck sand, "those tall, staggering remnants, those sloping columns of sunset!" Hessa ground them just shy of twilight, that the dreamt columns might be dimmed to the colour of skin darkened by the light behind it, and if they looked like slender necks, the fallen ones angled slant as a clavicle, the kind-eyed gentleman did not complain.

"Craft me a dream of wings and flight," murmured a shy young woman with gold-studded ears, "that I might soar above the desert and kiss the moon." Hessa ground a cabochon with her right hand while her left slid between her legs, rocking her to the memory of long fingers she built into feathers, sprouted to wings just as she moaned a spill of warm honey and weightlessness.

Afterward, she felt ashamed. She thought, surely someone would notice—surely, some dreamer would part the veils of ecstasy in their sleep and find her burning behind them. It felt, awkwardly, like trespass, but not because of the dreamers; rather, it seemed wrong to sculpt her nameless, braidless woman into the circlets she sold for money. It felt like theft, absurd though it was, and in the aftermath of her release, she felt guilty, too.

But she could not find her; she hardly knew how to begin to look. Perhaps she had been a traveller, after all, merely releasing her hair from a five-braided itch in the late afternoon; perhaps she had left the city, wandered to wherever it was she came from, some strange land where women wore their hair long and wild and lived lives of savage indolence, stretching out beneath fruit trees, naked as the sky—

The flush in her cheeks decided her. If she couldn't find her woman while waking, then what in the seven skies was her craft for, if not to find her in sleep?

⁓

Hessa had never crafted a dream for her own use. She tested her commissions, sometimes, to ensure their quality or correct an error, but she always recast the dream in fresh quartz and discarded the test stone immediately, throwing it into the bath of saltwater steam that would purify it for reworking into simple jewellery. It would not do, after all, for a silver necklace or brass ring to bear in it the echo of a stranger's lust. Working the hours she did, her sleep was most often profound and refreshing; if she dreamt naturally, she hardly ever remembered.

She did not expect to sleep well through the dream she purposed.

She closed shop for a week, took on no new commissions. She hesitated over the choice of stone; a dream crafted in white quartz could last for up to three uses, depending on the clarity of the crystal and the time she took in grinding it. But a dream crafted in amethyst could last indefinitely—could belong to her forever, as long as she wanted it, renewing itself to the rhythm of her thoughts, modulating its song to harmonise with her dream-desires. She had only ever crafted two dreams in amethyst, a matched set to be given as a wedding gift, and the sum she commanded for the task had financed a year's worth of materials and bought her a new lathe.

Reluctantly, she chose the white quartz. Three nights, that was all she would allow herself; three nights for a week's careful, loving labour, and perhaps then this obsession would burn itself out, would leave her sated. Three nights, and then no more.

She wondered if Salma had ever done anything of the sort.

⁓

For three days, she studied her only memory of the woman, of her standing framed in the doorway of Qahwat al Adraj, awash in dusty light; she remembered the cut of her coat, its colour, and the woman's eyes focusing on her, narrowing, quizzical. They were almost black, she thought, or so the light made them. And her hair, of course, her endless, splendid, dreadful hair, curling around her slim neck like a hand; she remembered the height of her, the narrowness that made her think of a sheathed sword, of a buried root, only her hair declaring her to be wild, impossible, strange.

Once the woman's image was perfectly fixed in her thoughts, Hessa began to change it.

Her stern mouth softened into hesitation, almost a smile; her lips parted as if to speak. Hessa wished she had heard her voice that day—she did not want to imagine a sound that was not truly hers, that was false. She wanted to shift, to shape, not to invent. Better to leave her silent.

Her mouth, then, and her height; she was probably taller than Hessa, but not in the dream, no. She had to be able to look into her eyes, to reach for her cheeks, to brush her thumb over the fullness of her lips before kissing them. Her mouth would be warm, she knew, and taste—

Here, again, she faltered. She would taste, Hessa, decided, of ripe mulberries, and her mouth would be stained with the juice. She would have fed them to her, after laughing over a shared joke—no, she would have placed a mulberry in her own mouth and then kissed her, yes, lain it on her tongue as a gift from her own, and that is why she would taste of mulberries as Hessa pressed a hand to the small of her back and gathered her slenderness against herself, crushed their hips together . . .

It took her five days to build the dream in her thoughts, repeating the sequence of her imagined pleasures until they wore grooved agonies into her mind, until she could almost savour the dream through her sleep without the aid of stone or circlet. She took a full day to cast the latter, and a full day to grind the stone to the axes of her dream, careful not to miss a single desired sensation; she set it carefully into its copper circlet.

Her fingers only trembled when she lifted it onto her head.

The first night left her in tears. She had never been so thoroughly immersed in her art, and it had been long, so long since anyone had approached her with a desire she could answer in kisses rather than craft. She ached for it; the braidless woman's body was like warm water on her skin, surrounded her in the scent of jasmine. The tenderness between them was unbearable; for all that she thirsted for a voice, for small sighs and gasps to twine with her own. Her hair was down soft, and the pleasure she took in wrapping it around her fingers left her breathless. She woke tasting mulberries, removed the circlet, and promptly slept until the afternoon.

The second night, she nestled into her lover's body with the ease of old habit, and found herself murmuring poetry into her neck, old poems in antique metres, rhythms rising and falling like the galloping warhorses they described. "I wish," she whispered, pressed against her afterward, raising her hand to her lips, "I could take you riding—I used to, when I was little. I would go riding to Maaloula with my family, where almond trees grow from holy caves, and where the wine is so black and sweet it is rumoured that each grape must have been kissed before being plucked to make it. I wish," and she sighed, feeling the dream leaving her, feeling the stone-sung harmony of it fading, "I wish I knew your name."

Strangeness, then—a shifting in the dream, a jolt, as the walls of the bedroom she had imagined for them fell away, as she found she could look at nothing but her woman's eyes, seeing wine in them, suddenly, and something else, as she opened her mulberry mouth to speak.

"Nahla," she said, in a voice like a granite wall. "My name is—"

Hessa woke with the sensation of falling from a great height, too shocked to move. Finally, with enormous effort, she removed the circlet, and gripped it in her hands for a long time, staring at the quartz. She had not given her a name. Was her desire for one strong enough to change the dream from within? All her dream devices were interactive to a small degree, but she always planned them that way, allowing room, pauses in the stone's song that the dreamer's mind could fill—she had not done so with her own, so certain of what she wanted, of her own needs. She had decided firmly against giving her a name, wanting so keenly to know the truth—and that voice, so harsh. That was not how she would have imagined her voice . . .

She put the circlet aside and rose to dress herself. She would try to understand it later that night. It would be her final one; she would ask another question, and see what tricks her mind played on her then.

But there would be no third night.

That afternoon, as Hessa opened her door to step out for an early dinner at Qahwat al Adraj, firm hands grasped her by the shoulders and shoved her back inside. Before she could protest or grasp what was happening, her braidless woman stood before her, so radiant with fury that Hessa could hardly speak for the pain it brought her.

"Nahla?" she managed.

"Hessa," she threw back in a snarl. "Hessa Ghaflan bint Aliyah bint Qamar bint Widad. Crafter of dreams. Ask me how I am here."

There were knives in Hessa's throat—she felt it would bleed if she swallowed, if she tried to speak. ". . . How?"

"Do you know"—she was walking, now, walking a very slow circle around her—"what it is like"—no, not quite around, she was coming toward her but as wolves did, never in a straight line, before they attacked, always slant—"to find your dreams are no longer your own? Answer me."

Hessa could not. This, now, felt like a dream that was no longer her own. Nahla's voice left her nowhere to hide, allowed her no possibility of movement. Finally, she managed something that must have looked enough like a shake of her head for Nahla to continue.

"Of course you wouldn't. You are the mistress here, the maker of worlds. I shall tell you. It is fascinating, at first—like being in another country. You observe, for it is strange to not be at the centre of your own story, strange to see a landscape, a city, an ocean, bending its familiarity toward someone not yourself. But then—then, Hessa—"

Nahla's voice was an ocean, Hessa decided, dimly. It was worse than the sea—it was the vastness that drowned ships and hid monsters beneath its sparkling calm. She wished she could stop staring at her mouth.

"—Then, you understand that the landscapes, the cities, the

oceans, these things are you. They are built out of you, and it is you who are bending, you who are changing for the eyes of these strangers. It is your hands in their wings, your neck in their ruins, your hair in which they laugh and make love—"

Her voice broke, there, and Hessa had a tiny instant's relief as Nahla turned away from her, eyes screwed shut. Only an instant, though, before Nahla laughed in a way that was sand in her own eyes, hot and stinging and sharp.

"And then you see them! You see them in waking, these people who bathed in you and climbed atop you, you recognise their faces and think you have gone mad, because those were only dreams, surely, and you are more than that! But you aren't, because the way they look at you, Hessa, their heads tilted in fond curiosity, as if they've found a pet they would like to keep—you are nothing but the grist for their fantasy mills, and even if they do not understand that, you do. And you wonder, why, why is this happening? Why now, what have I done—"

She gripped Hessa's chin and forced it upward, pushing her against one of her worktables, scattering a rainfall of rough-cut gems to the stone floor and slamming agony into her hip. Hessa did not resist anything but the urge to scream.

"And then," stroking her cheek in a mockery of tenderness, "you see a face in your dreams that you first knew outside them. A small, tired-looking thing you saw in a coffee house, who looked at you as if you were the only thing in the world worth looking at—but who now is taking off your clothes, is filling your mouth with berries and poems and won't let you speak, and Hessa, *it is so much worse*."

"I didn't know!" It was a sob, finally, stabbing at her as she forced it out. "I'm sorry, I'm so sorry—I didn't know, Nahla, that isn't how it works—"

"You made me into your *doll*." Another shove sent Hessa crumpling to the floor, pieces of quartz marking her skin with bruises and cuts. "Better I be an ancient city or the means to flight than your *toy*, Hessa! Do you know the worst of it?" Nahla knelt down next to her, and Hessa knew that it would not matter to her that she was crying, now, but she offered her tears up as penance all the same.

"The worst of it," she whispered, now, forefinger tracing one of Hessa's braids, "is that, in the dream, I wanted you. And I could not tell if it was because I found you beautiful, or because that is what you wanted me to do."

They stayed like that for some time, Hessa breathing through slow, ragged sobs while Nahla touched her head. She could not bring herself to ask, *do you still want me now?*

"How could you not know?" Nahla murmured, as she touched her, as if she could read the answer in Hessa's hair. "How could you not know what you were doing to me?"

"I don't control anything but the stone, I swear to you, Nahla, I promise," she could hear herself babbling, her words slick with tears, blurry and indistinct as her vision. "When I grind the dream into the quartz, it is like pressing a shape into wet clay, like sculpture, like carpentry—the quartz, the wax, the dop stick, the grinding plate, the copper and amber, these are my materials—these and my mind. I don't know how this happened, it is impossible—"

"That I should be in your mind?"

"That I, or anyone else, should be in yours. You aren't a material, you were only an image—it was never you, it couldn't have been, it was only—"

"Your longing," Nahla said, flatly. "Your wanting of me."

"Yes." Silence between them, then a long-drawn breath. "You believe me?"

A longer silence, while Nahla's fingers sank into the braids tight against Hessa's scalp, scratching it while clutching at a plaited line. "Yes."

"Do you forgive me?"

Slowly, Nahla released her, withdrew her hand, and said nothing.

Hessa sighed, and hugged her knees to her chest. Another moment passed; finally, thinking she might as well ask, since she was certain never to see Nahla again, she said, "Why do you wear your hair like that?"

"That," said Nahla, coldly, "is none of your business."

Hessa looked at the ground, feeling a numbness settle into her chest, and focused on swallowing her throat-thorns, quieting her breathing. Let her go, then. Let her go, and Hessa would find a way to forget this—although a panic rose in her, that after a lifetime of being taught how to remember, she had forgotten how to forget.

"Unless," Nahla continued, thoughtful, "you intend to make it your business."

Hessa looked up, startled. While she stared at her in confusion, Nahla seemed to make up her mind.

"Yes." She smirked, and there was something cruel in the bright twist of it. "I would be your apprentice! You'd like that, wouldn't you? To make my hair like yours?"

"No!" Hessa was horrified. "I don't—I mean—no, I wouldn't like that at all." Nahla raised an eyebrow as she babbled, "I've never had an apprentice. I was one only four years ago. It would not—it would not be seemly."

"Hessa." Nahla stood, now, and Hessa rose with her, knees shaky and sore. "I want to know how this happened. I want to learn"—she narrowed her eyes, and Hessa recoiled from what she saw there, but forgot it the instant Nahla smiled—"how to do it to you. Perhaps then, when I can teach you what it felt like, when I can silence you and bind you in all the ways I find delicious without asking your leave—perhaps then, I can forgive you."

They looked at each other for what seemed an age. Then, slowly, drawing a long, deep breath, Hessa reached for a large piece of rough quartz, and put it in Nahla's hand, gently closing her fingers over it.

"Every stone," she said, quietly, looking into her wine-dark eyes, "knows how to sing. Can you hear it?"

As she watched, Nahla frowned, and raised the quartz to her ear.

PIECES

Listen to the shooting ... Can you hear it? It's hammering on us like rain.

—Omar, a protestor in Homs

The world is wrong and I am wrung,
a bell of cloth dripping salt
into an earth too broken for roots.
I am a jumble, I am a heap,
a tangle of wires crosspurposed
and my voice is glass
and my voice is in the earth
and the rain is made of metal and mortar
and fire scorns water thin as air and the heat
melts skin. The world is wrong
and I am stung, I am raw to this wasp-air's buzz
to these teeth stacked like walls
against words, against tongues,
and I would tell these sons of men
something so shiningsharp that they would sing with it
hold the sun in a cup of their hands
but this glass voice breaks in my throat
and I would speak swallows with clear wings
to scrape an augury against the sky in splinters
but no one speaks glass.

My grandmother is a country I would know.
It is her name, her voice I hear
when I read this gold-cloth word
this sand-gold word, this sun-bright word

with its vowels askew in my alphabet,
this word of riches and gates, of grapes and roads,
of layers and music and dust. It is my grandmother's name
I hear breaking beneath numbers
beneath 200
beneath rain that heaves through bodies like grief
beneath forty-eight
and nineteen, and eighteen.
I will not speak of my name.

I will not speak of your countries
of this language we share
that is not glass. I will not speak
of your smoke
and your silence
and the bullets stitching purpose to our backs.

My voice is in pieces
I cannot swallow.
But if you would hear it
I will put a sliver in your eye
slide it stinging into place.
It is glass. See through it.
Change.

JOHN HOLLOWBACK AND THE WITCH

The witch had no name that he knew. John Hollowback found her house at the far end of a fallow field, browning with the fall: a small cottage of wattle and daub, with a thatched roof and a smoking chimney, nestled up against a forest of birch, poplar, and pine. He could see a well nearby, a tidy garden, and a store of seasoned wood stacked against the eastern wall.

It was a pretty place. He thought perhaps he was mistaken; it did not look like the home of a witch. Still, he walked to the door and knocked three times.

The woman who answered was most certainly a witch.

Her hair was dark, greasy, wisped in grey and falling messily out of a loose topknot; her skin was sun-browned and crinkled around her eyes, which were a strange, flashing blue. She did not look very old, but was hideous enough to be recognisable as one who practiced magic.

"What do you want?" Her voice was low, but clear.

"I want a whole back, instead of a hole in my back," he said, firmly.

She squinted at him, and gestured for him to turn around, poking at him curiously while he did.

Though he walked without a stoop or limp, John had a hollow in his back. Where spine and sinew were meant to make a bold line from neck to tailbone, they vanished instead into an oval cavity the size of a serving plate, lined with pale, soft skin.

"I used to be called John Turner," he said, bitterly. "Now folk call me Hollowback, like an old tree. Owls could nest in me."

She placed her hands against his shoulder blades, knocking against them like a door. She rapped her knuckles down his back until they met wood and the sound rang out hollow indeed. He winced.

"I made myself a board to cover the hole. I daren't be alone with women—"

"You're alone with me," she observed.

"You know what I mean. I have seen doctors, and they can do nothing. Can you help?"

She pulled her hands back, folded her arms, and considered him.

"Perhaps," she said. "Come in."

She led him towards the hearth and sat him down; he turned his back to her, lifted his shirt, and unfastened the leather bracers holding a thin sheet of wood against his hollow like a lid. He shivered as she felt around its edges, hissed when her fingers brushed the tender flesh within.

"I see," she murmured. "I see. You're missing a pound of flesh. Who did you cross?"

His shoulders slumped beneath her hands. "No one. I have no debts, and some money put by. A year ago I was to propose to my love; a year and a day ago I woke with a hollow in my back, and this frightened her away, and she never spoke to me again."

"Mm." She withdrew her hands. "A pity—it is difficult to restore that which has been taken by another."

"Then you cannot help me?"

"I did not say that." She tapped a thoughtful rhythm against his back. "But it will take some time. You will have to stay here for the duration. What have you brought with you?"

He lifted the flap of his bag and pulled out a leather-bound book.

"I thought you might value this, and take it as payment," he said, offering it to her. She raised a thick eyebrow, picked it up, and thumbed through it.

"It's blank," she said, looking at him curiously.

"It's magic," he said, "I think. Anything I try to write in it vanishes. I have no use for it, but I thought, perhaps, someone with your craft—"

"What else have you brought," she said, snapping it shut and tossing it aside. John flushed, swallowed, and poured out the rest of his bag.

He had packed sensibly: a change of clothing, some food, some money, along with his tools. But from among his belongings the witch singled out an apple, a comb, and a bit of string. John blinked; he had not packed them.

"These," she said, "will be of some use. Tomorrow we'll begin tending to your back. You are a woodworker, I see?"

John nodded.

"I will take my payment in trade, then. Go to sleep."

The witch sat in her garden while John slept, puffing a pipe. He didn't remember her; that much was clear. What he *did* remember remained to be seen.

She clicked her tongue in the language of bats until one swooped merrily around her head; she whispered with it a while, then watched as the bat wheeled away into the velvet dark.

John woke to the witch shaking him gruffly by the shoulder.

"We begin today," she said. "You'll do chores while it's light; at night, we will work together on your back. Is this fair by you?"

"Yes," he said, straightening, "yes, of course."

"Good. You must understand that once we begin this process, it will be difficult to stop. It is as if you are carrying a knife stuck in your back; if I pull it out, a dangerous gushing will result, and if you do not let me complete my work, it will go badly for you. I say this because it will be painful, and I will not hurt you without your consent. Do you understand?"

John felt suddenly unsure. "It will hurt?"

"Most likely. Great changes often do."

"Only, I don't remember it hurting when it happened."

The witch only stared at him, waiting.

John chewed his lip, then nodded. "And I only need to do chores? You don't want the book, or . . . a promise of . . ." He swallowed what might be an insulting assumption. ". . . some future thing?"

The witch looked more pitying than contemptuous. She reached up to clap him on the shoulder.

"John Hollowback," she said, "you have absolutely nothing I could possibly want."

⁓

On that first day, John swept the witch's floors, scoured her pots, drew water from her well, and scouted a space outdoors to set up a spring-pole lathe. She'd said she expected trade, but nothing else; he wanted to be prepared. By the time the witch called him in, he had most of it done, and had worked up an honest sweat; she'd set out a robust dinner for the two of them, bread and cheese and a thick vegetable stew. They ate in silence—not quite companionable, but not awkward, either.

Once they'd finished, John cleared the table and washed up; the witch, meanwhile, set the apple on the table, and waited for him to join her.

"Take off your shirt," she said, "and your board, and lie down on your belly."

He did as he was told, if reluctantly; it was not easy to show his naked back. He found he was less ashamed about it with the witch, though; perhaps because she wore her own ugliness so brazenly, he didn't so much mind his own. Wherever he came face-to-face with people they found him handsome: he was after all tall, with straight teeth and a small nose, high cheekbones and honeyed hair. But when he turned his back, he knew people shuddered at the shape of him, whispered about the odd way his shirt hung off his shoulders, a strange sag at his belt.

He propped his chin up on his folded arms and gazed into the dimming embers of the fire while the witch moved around behind him.

"I'm going to make a scrying bowl of your hollow," she said, "by painting it black, and filling it with water. While I do this, I want you to tell me the story of this apple."

She held it out to him. He frowned.

"It's just an apple. I must've packed it for a snack and forgotten about it."

"It spoke to me," she said, simply, "from among your things. You seem to be missing more than flesh, John Hollowback—there are memories you carry outside your body, and I don't think you'll be whole again until you've recalled them." She sat down next to him on a low stool, swirling a paint brush through a pungent stone jar, and began applying its contents to his back.

He hissed—it was cold—then wrinkled his nose, annoyed. "That's nonsense. I'll grant I don't remember my hollowing, but I've a decent memory in general, and—"

"Eat it."

He blinked. "What?"

"Eat the apple. Take a bite."

He was rather full from dinner, but he shrugged his shoulders, parted his lips, lifted it to his mouth—and stopped, suddenly wracked with nausea. He gasped, sick-drool pooling around his tongue, and turned away from it, panting—but could not drop it, though he felt it growing warm in his hand, echoing something thumping hard in his chest.

"You can't eat it," said the witch, her voice rougher than he would have liked, "any more than you can eat your arm. But you can tell me the story of it." She laid another long, thick line down the bowl of his back while he caught his breath.

John turned the apple over in his hands. It was, he thought, a lovely specimen, red and round, its stem flying a single leaf like a flag; it looked just-picked, carried the scent of the orchard with it, the fizzy smell of ferment rising up from fruit crushed underfoot. Nothing in his bag had broken or bruised its surface; he owned as that was odd. But a story? The story of the apple was that it was a mystery, though the more he looked at it, the more he cupped it in his hands, the more he felt an unaccountable tenderness welling up in him.

He flinched as the witch poured a pitcher of cool water into his back, exhaled as she stirred her finger through it.

"I see," she murmured, "a great many trees, and among them a wagon, brightly coloured. There are women picking apples, but the wagon—"

"Oh!" said John, suddenly. "Of course, yes—that was when I first met her. Lydia, my—" He grimaced. "She was working, bringing in the fruit, and she was singing . . ."

The witch said nothing, but slowed her stirring. John found himself tugging at the thread of memory—perhaps this was what she meant, by telling the story? The apple reminded him of something, and he shared it? He groped his way to a better beginning.

"I was travelling with a troupe of players—not a player myself, of course, but I'd make their sets, mend the boards they trod, and they gave me a share of the take. William and Janet, they were married, and Brigid, she wasn't their daughter but may as well have been. We travelled in a caravan that was both advertisement and stage—or, well, they all did, being a family. I usually followed after them on a mule, stopping in towns to ply my own trade and sleep in a bed before catching them up at the next stop—more comfortable for everyone that way, the wagon was only so big.

"Well, we were setting up in this orchard with the farmer's permission, and this girl was up a ladder—she was fine enough to look at, but her voice was something else. She was singing, leading the other workers in a song, call and response, and it was like hearing a lark among crows. I stopped setting up, stopped everything just to listen to her. And when the song was done I strode up to her and said as how I'd loved her singing, and her voice was a gift, and why was she picking fruit when she could be travelling the country and sharing out the gold of her music? And she blushed and smiled and plucked an apple from a branch near her cheek and held it out to me, and said that was very kind, but she was only a country lass. But we got to talking, and I brought the players out to meet her, and she watched our show. And that did it. She was off with us the next morning."

The water in his back felt warm now, not unpleasantly.

"Give me the apple, John," said the witch, quietly; she coaxed it from his hand—he found it hard to release—and then rolled it around the edge of his hollow. A ringing rose in his ears, a pain, a sharp slicing of grief—and then water sloshed over the edge of his hollow and he cried out, spun quickly to face her, scuttling back and away on his palms and making a mess of the floor.

The witch looked at him coolly.

"There. That's one." She looked from him to the puddle on the floor, and stood up slowly. "Enough for now, I think. Mop that up. Don't bother putting your board on tomorrow—it won't fit. Best give your back a little room to breathe."

She walked out to the garden, leaving John gasping, reaching around to touch the familiar contours of his hollow—and finding, instead, an inch more solid back than he'd had before.

The next morning, John woke late; the witch had let him sleep in. He was glad of it: he felt sore and stiff throughout his body, as if he'd spent a long night drinking. He stretched, and scratched, and reached cautiously towards his hollow. His shoulders slumped in relief when he found his new flesh still in place. He looked around for a mirror, and saw one hanging on the wall; steeling himself against the possibility that it might do him some mischief, he approached it and tried to catch a glimpse of his back in it.

The hollow was certainly smaller—but a thin black ring marked its previous circumference. He frowned. Perhaps it would fade in time.

He could hear the witch puttering out in the garden, and dragged himself to the bread and cheese she'd left on the table—next to the leather-bound book she'd refused from him as payment. Or had she accepted it? She was an odd one—she spoke plainly, but John felt there was much she didn't say.

As he munched his breakfast, he decided there was no harm in opening the book.

Then he choked.

The first few pages had writing on them. Not just any writing; the story he'd told the witch last night.

Well, he thought, that made sense; who better than a witch to write in a magic book? Perhaps that had always been its purpose—to be a witch's grimoire, inscribed with spells.

Funny that she'd write his own story in it. Odd, too, to see his story laid out by another, in writing. It seemed, at a glance, much longer than his own telling.

He skimmed over the memory of apples, and felt, again, the pang of losing Lydia, the sting of betrayal, the anger and shame of it. There had been so much promise at first, and then, at the end, no hint of anything amiss until she was gone.

"Good, you're awake," said the witch, standing in the doorway, tugging off her gardening gloves. John startled, slammed the book shut, and turned to her equal parts furtive, guilty, and defiant.

She did not seem to notice. "The day's getting away from us. Do you need me to make you a list, or can you get on all right just looking around at what needs doing?"

She made him a list, in the end, and once he'd chopped wood and hauled water to her satisfaction, he turned back to finishing his lathe.

He thought he might make the witch a bowl, as a small joke, since she'd made one of him. He found a likely birch log, split it in half, and began chipping out a rough shape. He'd just gotten as far as fitting it onto the lathe when the witch came out to see him, and he noticed the hour gone late and golden around him.

The witch looked at the lathe with frank curiosity. "I see you've not been idle."

John's hollow back straightened somewhat. He took pride in his work.

She stepped around to his side. "Would you show me? Or is it a trade secret?"

John demonstrated the mechanism—how the treadle tugged the pole down and spun the wood to be shaped in one direction, then the other as it released. "You only cut on the downstroke," he said, "slowly, carefully. Then it springs back up—it's called reciprocating action—and you push down again, until it takes the shape you want."

"Fascinating," she said, quietly. "Very clever. Does the wood ever break, or crack?"

"Not if it's sufficiently green, seen to by a steady hand."

"I see," she said. "And is this light enough to work by?"

"No," he admitted. "I should leave off for tonight."

"Wise. And so shall I—I don't think you're entirely recovered from yesterday. Come and have something to eat."

That evening, their meal together was more genial; the witch asked about his back, whether he'd felt any pain after their ritual.

"No," he said, "but there's a black ring..."

She shrugged. "Sutures leave scars. It's all part of the process. I can't undo what happened to you; I can only help mend it."

She asked, then, about his memories of travelling on the road.

It had been a bright and venturesome time; they'd performed in villages and taverns, but also led the occasional masque or revelry in a grand country hall. Their summers they spent on the road; in winter they sought the shelter of familiar fields, farmers and sometimes gentry glad of the entertainment during long, cold nights.

It was while holed up together that they came to know each other best, he and Lydia. Her arrival had expanded the group's repertoire: where before they'd performed scraps of entertaining miscellanies, told stories, made use of John's modest skills in puppetry, now they had a full complement of players—though it meant Brigid usually took on trouser roles to play a young lover opposite Lydia's ingenue, or else a puckish troublemaker needling William and Janet's grumpier elder roles.

But Lydia was indisputably the star.

"Did you never perform with them?" asked the witch, pouring them both a fragrant tea after they'd eaten.

"I did before—if they needed someone to be a prop, or a mark, or to move a puppet. I'm no actor, I know that—hard not to when you travel with those who have the gift. But once they had Lydia, it was better to keep to making and mending. She cast a long shadow."

"Were you jealous?" she asked, with a frankness that felt like a slap.

"No," he said, staring at her. She held his gaze. Eventually he looked away. "No. But Brigid was."

The witch chuckled, and John frowned. But she stood and asked him to tidy up after their meal, putting an end to the matter, then walked out into the garden. He was asleep before she returned.

⸺

The next morning John woke early, but not earlier than the witch, and found a bowl of porridge laid out for him as well as some late plums. The leather-bound book was there, too.

JOHN HOLLOWBACK AND THE WITCH

He watched it while he ate. He looked out toward the garden, where the witch likely was.

He pulled the book towards him, opened it, and read.

Lydia picked apples and sang as she worked; she loved hearing her voice strong and high, feeling her call pull in a chorus of responses, as if she cast a net to catch her fellows' breath. But when she stopped, she felt eyes on her, and turned to see a tall, thin young man staring.

"That's a terrible ladder," he said. "It's dangerous, you could fall. Let me fix it."

Lydia laughed, for the ladder had borne her weight without wobbling all season, but she hopped down and let him have his way. As he shook his head and set about tightening the rungs, he said, "You have the most beautiful voice I've ever heard. And I've heard plenty. I'm John, what's your name?"

"Lydia," she said, smiling. "Thank you, that's kind."

"No, it's just true."

She asked if he was with the caravan of players, and he said he was. Her eyes shone, and she said she was looking forward to the show, that she loved the music and stories; he paused in his work, and said he could take her to meet the players, if she wanted.

She did want, very much.

She met William, Janet, and Brigid in short order; John introduced her as the voice of the orchard, and she rolled her eyes, but said she did love to sing. Brigid's eyes caught hers, and she asked about her favourite songs, and they fell to talking like they'd known each other for years but had not seen each other for more, familiar and starved for each other, while William and Janet exchanged fond looks and John sat silent and looked at everyone apart from himself.

John tasted copper before realizing he'd bitten through his lip. He shut the book, then opened it, fingers trembling. Then he shut it again.

How dare the witch? He'd come to her with his hollow, his history, and she had made of it—whatever this was, a fanciful embroidery, some kind of cruel taunt.

Had he even said he fixed the ladder? He recalled, now, that he'd tightened the rungs, but it hadn't seemed worth mentioning. Was that really the first thing he'd said to Lydia?

He shoved his porridge aside and stormed out to the lathe.

⌒

The work soon soothed him. His world narrowed in focus to angles and pressure and speed, the beauty of wood smoothed and shaped, every rough part sheared off into a tangle of delicate blonde curls. By the time the witch came out to find him, the finished bowl gleamed.

"Here," said John, stiffly. "Trade."

The witch raised her eyebrows at him, and took the proffered bowl, turning it in her hands. "It's lovely. Well done."

John flushed, but looked away. The witch eyed him, then said, lightly, "I know just what to do with it. Come with me."

He followed her into her garden, where she wandered, stooped, cut lettuces and herbs with a short sharp knife. Whatever she cut, she placed in the bowl, until it was heaped with brilliant, tender greenery.

"Walk with me, John," she said. "We'll not be long."

"Where are we going?"

"To visit a neighbour. Now, what's the matter?"

He scowled. "Nothing."

"It's the wrong season for lemons," she said, "but you look like you've been feasting on little else. And you didn't clean up after breakfast; that porridge'll be crusted to its bowl like a barnacle."

He rolled his eyes. "Pardon me for having made you a better one."

The witch stopped walking, and looked up at him. Her eyes flashed—literally, magically—and he looked away, fuming.

"John Hollowback," she said, calmly, "you'll keep a civil tongue in your head when you speak to me, or else you'll keep a home in your back for owls. Is that understood?"

He chewed his lip. "Yes."

"We made a bargain, and I have asked very little of you. Tell me what's wrong or keep your own council, but do not think to insult me or my crockery with your backhanded foolishness while accepting my hospitality. Shame on you."

She walked on, and reluctantly, he followed.

Eventually they came to a cottage, and were warmly received by the couple inside: a woman, heavily pregnant, her husband beaming solicitously alongside her.

"I brought these for the cravings," said the witch, pressing the bowl into the woman's hands. "Make a salad of them, they'll be good for you." She looked to John, and smiled. "John here made the bowl."

John stood awkwardly by while the couple gushed their thanks; they pressed a small loaf and a jar of bramble jam on them, which the witch handed John to carry. Mercifully she declined their offer of dinner. They began their walk back in silence.

"I made that bowl for you," said John, who wanted to be angry, but was mostly tired. The witch shrugged.

"And I traded it for bread and jam. I did say I'd take my payment in trade." She looked at him, levelly. "And that I wanted nothing from you. I always mean what I say, John."

"I thought," said John, who wanted to be vicious, but wasn't up to the task, "that witches hated giving up their greens. That they punished people for taking from their gardens. We did a whole show about it once."

She chuckled. "And why not? Everyone wants to see a witch punish someone for stealing from her. A witch is a kind of justice in the world. It makes for a fine story. No one wants to admit the truth, for all it stares them plainly in the face."

"What's that?"

"Steal from a woman long enough, and a witch is what she'll become."

They'd reached the cottage. John drew a deep breath.

"I'm sorry," he said, grudgingly, "for being rude. But I saw what you'd written in the book, and I didn't like it."

He didn't like, either, the pitying way the witch looked at him now.

"John," she said, "I've not written anything in that book."

She laid him down shirtless in front of the hearth again, painted another layer of black into his hollow. She handed him the comb, poured water into the bowl of him, and propped the leather-bound book open to a fresh page where he could see it.

"I believe I understand," she said, "what has happened to you, and the way it came about. But it's a little like trying to rebuild a tree from a pile of wood shavings. There is so much you don't remember, and it's necessary that you do. So: tell me the story of the comb."

She began stirring the water in his back again.

John looked at the comb: it was very elegant, long-handled, and decorated with flowering vines carved out of the wood. He recognized his own work.

"I made this for her," he said. "I made her lots of things—but I could say they were for the troupe, if I were building scenery that would show her particularly well, or making improvements to the wagon. But I made her this as a gift, from me to only her, and she let me brush her hair with it, and I knew then that she loved me, to let me stand so close to her."

The water in his back heated up much more quickly this time, and less comfortably. He shifted on his belly, and looked from the comb in his hands to the open book in front of him.

It was filling with writing. He squinted to read it.

John prided himself on introducing people to each other. He was no great performer, but he liked to say that he was the trusses that held up the stage, that he carried them all on his back. Sometimes he would ride ahead of the wagon and make connections through his woodworking—connections which he then leveraged into performance opportunities—and sometimes he would hang back after the show to glean gossip and carry that back to the group. He had an uncanny knack for placing himself between people, and resented the existence of any closeness that did not widen to admit him.

He resented Janet and William's direction; he resented Brigid and Lydia's friendship; he resented Lydia's passion for performing, and the audience's passion for her. And the more he resented them, the more he plied them with gifts, words and wood and wooing coated in the venom of his need.

⁓

John hissed. The water in his back steamed. "It's not true," he gasped, "it's not true."

"Tell me what is, then," said the witch quietly, stirring the while.

"I loved them." His lip trembled. "I loved them all."

But he looked back to the book, and read.

⁓

To William and Janet, he brought a pair of beautifully turned bowls, and while they ate together he spoke grave rumours of unfriendly villages ahead, dislike of outsiders, a dwindling of prospects leading to a hard winter.

"Some say it's unnatural for women to play men on the stage," he said, his eyes soft and sad, "and mutter dark things to each other. Honestly, I fear for Brigid—but I'm sure these words will pass like weather, it's probably nothing."

And William and Janet paled, and reached for each other's hands.

To Brigid, he brought hand-carved dice, and played games 'til they were deep in their cups, and spoke of Lydia's talent, her brilliance.

"But I worry," he said, "that she'll only ever be thought of as one half of a pair—that she'll be stamped like a coin into one role until she's spent."

And Brigid frowned, and John looked contrite, and said, "It's not that I think you're smothering her," and paused, "but I do think she feels smothered."

And Brigid looked stricken, and the next morning went with a pounding head to have a word with William and Janet, and was soon visiting nearby family for a spell while Lydia's heart shook to see her go.

To Lydia, he brought a hand-carved comb, beautifully wrought with flowers and vines, and offered to dress her hair before she mounted the stage, as Brigid used to do.

"You know," he said, combing her long, bright hair, "when you stand on stage you shine."

She smiled softly. "Thank you, John."

"But sometimes," he said, "you shine so bright that it hurts to look at you. You're like a small sun, and lesser stars can't be seen when you're out."

Lydia's throat hurt. "Does it bother you?"

"No, no, of course not." He paused. "But I think it bothers Brigid."

And Brigid put distance between them, and Lydia dimmed herself, until soon they couldn't see each other at all.

And so John made room for himself.

John hardly felt the witch take the comb from him, stunned by the words and the gulf they opened in his chest. But when she began running it along the outside of his hollow, he screamed: it burned, as if the comb's teeth seared grooves around his bowl-back's rim. The water that spilled over the edges of him scalded; he panted, then drew his knees in close to his chest and wept while the witch watched.

"That's two," she said, low and gruff, and left him.

The next morning, John woke to voices in the garden. The witch—and one other. He tried to rise—and groaned, his body a patchwork of pains and aches, then groaned more deeply as he remembered the source of it all.

The visitor sounded agitated, but he couldn't make out the words. The witch's voice came clear.

"I'm sorry, but I'm busy now. Come back tonight, and we'll speak more of it then."

She came in a moment later, looked at him, then busied herself in brewing a pot of mint tea while he found his way to a seat.

He stared into nothing while she poured him a cup.

"What must you think of me," he whispered, "to hear me say what I do, and then read what's written in that book?"

The witch shrugged. She poured herself some tea and sat down. "What do you think of yourself?"

"I hate it," he said. "I don't recognize the man in those pages. It isn't how I remember it."

"But you didn't remember any of it, at first," she said, lifting her cup, sniffing it. "All you remembered was losing your lover."

John kept silent. He blew gently on his tea.

"I don't want to wait until tonight," he said, finally. "I'd like to get it over with. Can we do this by daylight?"

The witch sipped her tea as she looked at him. It struck him, suddenly, that she wasn't ugly at all—he couldn't remember how he'd thought that.

"We can. But it will hurt you terribly."

He looked into his cup, and nodded. "I know."

Laid out on his belly again while the witch painted his back, he twirled the string this way and that between his thumbs and forefingers.

"I used this," he said, his voice a shallow croak, "to measure her finger for a ring. I wanted to make her a wooden one—I was going to ask her to marry me. But then everything went wrong."

"How? What happened?"

John's throat worked, but he couldn't remember. He shook his head. "She was gone when I woke. They all were."

The witch stirred the waters in his back—smaller and smaller circles, he felt, as his flesh had filled in, though he could take no joy in it—and said, "I see a great hall done up with harvest revelry: sheafs of wheat, garlands of asters, great rounds of braided bread."

"Yes," said John, "the troupe's last performance. William and Janet had decided . . . they'd"—he drew a deep breath—"they'd lost their taste for travel, and the take wasn't what it used to be. There was no better time to ask Lydia to marry me—I'd look after her, and we could be our own troupe together, if she wanted. I could set up shop in a town, she could sing in a proper theatre—I would've built her one from the ground up, I knew enough of the right people. I had something to offer her, and she had nothing to lose—"

"Because you'd taken everything from her?"

John gritted his teeth. "I never *took* anything from anyone. I had nothing, I came from nothing, I built everything I had for myself.

I never forced anyone to do anything they didn't want to. I only ever tried to help."

He glared up at the book, daring it to contradict him. For a moment, nothing appeared.

Then black ink bloomed from the blank pages and sank John's heart to his stomach.

༄

The night of the final performance, Brigid brought her mother to see the show, and to meet John and Lydia, of whom she'd heard much spoken. John was genial and spoke expansively, praised everyone but himself; Lydia smiled, demure, said little.

Brigid's mother looked at them together: how John's arm wrapped too tightly around Lydia whenever anyone else was around—how she wilted near him—how, if ever his gaze went elsewhere, if he were called away, she seemed to relax, to straighten, to smile more easily and speak more freely.

She looked, too, at her own daughter: how she floated away from the friend she would not cease praising in her visits home, but orbited her like a moth near a lantern.

She saw that some sick magic was at work.

"Lydia," she said, "would you lend me this fine fellow of yours? John, I noticed some odd carvings under the seats here, I wondered if you could tell me about them."

And John, flattered, turned his back on Brigid and Lydia, whose eyes found each other, and whose hands soon followed, and who, haltingly and in a daze, remembered how to speak.

༄

Tears brimmed in John's eyes and he knuckled them away as he turned his face from the book. "You can't hold me responsible for them drifting apart!"

The witch stirred his waters placidly. "Who are you talking to, John?"

"Look, if they'd really loved each other, nothing I said or did could have changed that. I only wanted them to love me too, as I loved them!"

"How did you love them, then?"

"They were everything to me," he said, fiercely. "They were my life, all of them together, and I was just—a tool. A handyman. I wanted to be everything to at least one person."

"Reciprocating action," she said. "Isn't that what you called it? Your work with the lathe. You'd pull her to you, and cut away what you didn't like, and then if she bounced away she was less—until you caught her again, and cut and carved until she fit in the palm of your hand."

"*I* discovered her! *I* made her a star!"

"What happened with the string, John?"

"I don't know! The performance went well—Lydia was more dazzling than she'd been in ages, she was pressed on all sides afterward by admirers, and I couldn't find her for hours. But we were all going to sleep together in the hall that night, after the show, so I just waited. I waited a long time into the night, and when she came in it was her and Brigid together, and I couldn't . . . I didn't want to interrupt, so I pretended to be asleep until they were. And then I got up, and—"

He gasped as the water in his back began to boil. The witch pulled her finger back a second before it burned, shook the heat out. "Go on, John."

"I crept closer—I tried to tie the string around her finger without her waking, but—she did, and—"

༄

"What are you doing?" she hissed, snatching her hand from his, looking at the string in horror. "What's this?"

"Nothing—nothing, go back to sleep—"

"Is this a spell?" She tugged at the string on her finger, in a panic, in a rage, as Brigid stirred beside her. "Is this *how you—what are you doing* to me*?"*

"Lydia, please," he said, finding his way to one knee, looking at her, his eyes large and beseeching as a dog's, "I wanted to ask you to marry—"

The string around her finger glowed like metal in a forge, then snapped and sizzled away to nothing. Lydia herself began to glow, as if stars melted into her veins, and rose up from her blankets, rose further still, until she floated above him, her hair high and wild as the lightning, and the air around her crackled with power.

"Liar," she hissed, and the word burned bright as her hair. "Liar! You've tried to cut me and bind me like wheat all this time!" And she spoke back at him every truth she'd untwisted from his words, every piece of her he'd taken while seeming to give her gifts, every day he'd ruined with his sad jealous eyes reproaching her for hurting him with her happiness.

And as John watched a witch being born, he felt a great gouging at his back, as if a giant hand in one single stroke had sheared spine and flesh and blood and skin from him, and out from the coring of his body tumbled an apple, a comb, a piece of string, and a book, and he fell down among them in a swoon.

When he woke up, it was midday, and the hall was empty. He picked up the objects around him without seeing them, put them in a bag, and carried them with him for a year and a day.

⸙

He screamed his throat raw as the witch rolled the string into his hollow. The water turned to vapour; the thick paint on his back smoked and peeled. Bones jutted beneath his blackened skin like mountain peaks, twisted like serpents coiling, cracked and rumbled like a thundering sky—but settled, finally, solid and sound as good joinery. He panted and sobbed while the witch rubbed circles along his newly filled back—whole now, but for a small gap an inch wide and a few inches deep, surrounded by three black rings.

"Good, John," she whispered. "Well done."

⸙

John slept the day through. As the hour grew long and blue, the witch sat in her garden with her pipe, waiting for her visitor.

"I can't believe," came a voice bitter and hot, "that you would help him. After everything he did to us."

"Sit, Lydia," she said, gesturing to another stool. "How was your journey? How's Brigid?"

Lydia narrowed her eyes. "She told me not to murder you. How could you?"

The witch shrugged. "He came to my door and asked for help."

"And that's it, then? He's whole now, and anyone who looks at him will see just another smiling charming man and not know to shun him? It wasn't for you to fix him!"

The witch raised an eyebrow. "Did you want the task?"

"Of course not."

"Or Brigid, or who, then? Be honest, now."

Lydia's eyes flashed—literally, magically. "I didn't want him fixed at all. He doesn't deserve it."

"Ah, there we come to it. And that's why I did it." The witch held her gaze. "For you to carry less of it. For him to carry more of it."

Lydia's face twisted in disgust, and she shook her head. But she sat down, and stared out into the darkness.

"I'll never forget what you said that night," she said, her voice full of burrs. *"A witch is a kind of justice in the world.* And here you are, undoing it."

The witch tapped the ash from her pipe.

"When you came into your power," she said, "what he'd done to you came back to him fourfold. But that was the end of your story with him. You began a new one; so too should he, with the remembrance of all he did written into his body."

"Why tell me, though? You must have known I'd hate it."

"I wasn't asking permission. But I thought you should know." She pinched herbs from a pouch and packed them into her pipe. "I wasn't going to let him become a secret I kept from you."

Lydia breathed deeply, and exhaled slowly. "I won't see him, or speak to him. Not ever again."

"Nor should you."

"You don't want me to?"

"No. I'd put seven seas between you first." She tilted her head towards the cottage door, listening. "In fact, you'd best be away; I hear him stirring. Give my love to Brigid."

Lydia looked towards the cottage door. Then she hugged the witch to her, kissed her cheek, and said, "I will."

She left. The witch went back inside.

John was awake and waiting for her—still pale and shaken from the pain, but calm. She crouched down next to him, took his temperature with her wrist against his brow.

"You're Brigid's mother," he said, quietly. "I didn't remember you."

"Hard to remember a witch," she said, amiably, "at the best of times."

"You knew who I was from the beginning."

"I did."

"And you helped me?"

She shrugged. "You asked for help. I'm not sure you're happier now than when you came, though, are you?"

He chuckled bleakly. "No."

"Then perhaps all I did was enjoy seeing you punished."

"May I stay?" His eyes were wide and soft. "I'll keep helping, I could make you chairs and spoons—"

"Absolutely not." The witch's gaze was sharp, and he flinched from it. "You're good at your craft, John. But people aren't blocks of wood for you to turn to your liking, and you've not quite learned that yet, in your bones." She stood, and walked over to the leather-bound book that lay closed now. "Have you tried writing in it since coming here? It might keep your words now, if you choose them carefully."

She found him ink and a quill. He sat with it a while, reading through every word, feeling his memories shift and spike and settle like the objects in his back.

He tried writing "Lydia," and it wouldn't stay. He tried writing "I wish," and it wouldn't stay, the ink swallowed by the page like a pebble by a pond.

He wrote, "I'm sorry," and the words stared back at him like eyes, and stayed.

He closed the book.

"I'm ready," he said, and handed it to the witch. She took it, turned him around, and angled the book carefully at what remained of his hollow.

It slid into place like an ending.

FLORILEGIA; OR, SOME LIES ABOUT FLOWERS

You can't have flowers made of claws.
—Alan Garner, *The Owl Service*

Her first memory is a loss of sun. Where there was warmth on the white crown of her head, there is now cold shade, and two round shapes blotting out her light, blinking.

Her second memory is a loss of thorns. Where she was sharp, fierce, protected, she feels now smooth, soft, and vulnerable, pressed against green and yielding grass.

Her third memory is a loss of height. She has never felt so far from the sky, so lost to the wind.

Threaded through all this, the loss of roots unspools in her like a scream, the loss of rain, the loss of earth, the loss of everything she knows as food, and she has never, not in the bleakest midwinter or the driest midsummer, felt so hungry.

Small wonder, then, that she kissed Lleu Llaw Gyffes at their first meeting.

She was only trying to eat him.

Blodeuwedd lies naked in the orchard earth, trying to grow roots.

The day is miserable and gray, but not cold; her skin warms the mud beneath it. She breathes in long, deep breaths, and wills the hunger blooming in her centre to still.

The hunger is always an ache, a shadow pushing against the inside of her skin. Today it is her head that hurts, her brow that pulses with pain; other days it is her calf, her breast, her belly.

She has been a year in the house of Lleu Llaw Gyffes, and has learned many things: how to run a household; how to use needle and thread; how to receive guests. She eats meat fresh from her husband's hunting, drinks beer from her women's brewing, listens to music from minstrels praising the great lords and wizards making marvels of the countryside. She has learned to endure her husband's presence and make use of his absence, and she has learned to treat the hunger in her like a sucking wound.

But she does not know how to cure it. All she can do is pack it with wet earth, fragrant air, and grit her teeth against being turned inside out.

Lying in the orchard helps. Whenever Lleu leaves—as he often does—to hunt, or fight, or do whatever else men do, she slips from the house to find a corner where none will seek her for the space of an hour. Whether it is the touch of loam against her body, or the fact that it is hers alone, her secret, she can't say—but it helps.

Bees thrill to her fingertips, buzz their puzzlement at her shape. She opens her mouth and lets them sip from her there, tastes the pollen on their dainty legs. She imagines the fields they've scoured for her; she imagines them carrying the wetness of her tongue over the walls, across meadows and arbours, spreading her across distances farther than her eyes or voice can reach.

The thought trembles in her like light on water, and she feels something release. She licks her lips and lies there, perfectly still, and does not stir when it begins to rain.

On their wedding night, Lleu told her the story of his birth, and hers too.

"... and when Arianrhod was made to leap over my uncle Math's wand, I tumbled out of her, and my uncle Gwydion scooped me up. But because I was proof of her shame, my mother, Arianrhod, decreed that I would never have a name unless she named me, nor be armed unless she armed me, nor wed to any woman of any race on earth. But my uncles were cleverer than she. Between them they tricked her into naming me without knowing who I was; they tricked her into arming me by making her fear invasion. But last, and best, my uncle Gwydion gathered the blossoms of oak, meadowsweet, and broom, and he shaped them into you, Blodeuwedd, and that is how we come to be married, my love, and why we lie together this night."

His eyes were like clouds that bore no rain, like stone begging to be broken through.

It sounds, she thought, *as if your uncles forced you on the body of Arianrhod, and when she tried to deny you, made me for you to force yourself on.*

But his hand on her arm had the strength of a gale, and she knew this thing, this man, could kill her as easily as his uncles had plucked her from the fields—unless she swayed with him, kept quiet, and smiled.

All her words bent into a flower budding from her tongue. She bit it back. When he kissed her, she filled his mouth with blood and petals, planted her silence in his body like a seed.

⸻

"Blodeuwedd? Blodeuwedd!"

She hears the name as if from a distance, as if filtered through dark cloth. She opens her eyes: Lleu, in the mizzle and the grey, his face flushed so hot she fancies she can see steam rising from his cheeks.

Her peace shrivels, and her head pounds with pain.

"What are you doing, woman? What were you thinking? You'll catch your death—"

He drapes her in the wet, muddy robes she'd shed, scoops her up off the ground and covers her with his body.

She lets him. She does not ask why he's returned earlier than expected, and makes herself very small in his arms.

"The shame of it, my lady, if anyone but I saw you thus—"

She looks at him, and looks at him, and thinks, *You don't see me.*

"What's this," he says, lifting a gloved hand to her brow. "Have you bruised yourself, my love? Best you go to bed and warm up. I'll call my uncles—"

"No," she says, with her whole body. "No, no need to trouble them," in a voice like the rain. She reaches up, twines her fingers through his, and slowly draws his hand back from her cheek, smiling. "I will rest, as you say." Then, mechanically, "It is good to see you home so soon."

He relaxes. "I only returned to accompany a visiting scholar from the abbey, and must leave again quickly to make up the time."

She nods, winces as he kisses the dark space on her brow. It darkens further.

He sees nothing in her green and gold-flecked eyes of how much she longs to tear his gentle face apart.

⸺

A month after the wedding, Lleu's uncles, Math and Gwydion, came to visit.

Blodeuwedd felt the candles flicker at their arrival, remembered her world dimming in the shadow of their heads. But she received them as a lady should, calling for food and drink and entertainment, then drew back with women's work between her hands.

"Are you happy, Lleu?" asked Math, as if Blodeuwedd weren't there. "Is she everything a wife should be?"

Lleu, who was indeed happy, smiled. "Indeed; she is beautiful, gracious to guests, and keeps the household in order."

"That's as it should be," said Gwydion gruffly. "That's how we made her. Meadowsweet, useless but for its scent; broom for humility and neatness; oak for hospitality."

"I always wondered about that," said Lleu thoughtfully. "Has not the broom thorns, and the oak great strength?"

Blodeuwedd's hands hovered over her embroidery.

Math laughed. "Aye, Nephew, but we only took the flowers of each. Soft and pretty and fragrant they were, like cutting roses off at the head. Whoever heard of a blossom with claws?"

She pushed the needle through the fabric on her lap, and said nothing.

⸺

Lleu leaves again; meanwhile the purpling on her forehead spreads across her pale skin like a storm, and the pain hoods her eyes. She dresses her hair to cover it, and goes to the library.

It too is an orchard, after a fashion—full of dead trees, dead skins, dead plants, dead insects mounted on pins. She feels this in common with them. The library offers a different comfort: if she can no longer grow roots to sate her hunger, perhaps she can learn to die. To catch her death, as her husband says, by lingering with the dead.

Often she comes here to read of Arianrhod—gleaning, from half mentions in tales and ballads, some sense of the mother-in-law she has never met. Arianrhod is almost as much a mother to her as to Lleu, after all; Blodeuwedd would not exist without her interdiction forbidding wives. But she has never been able to hate Arianrhod for that—only to feel, deep where her roots aren't, a fury that her life is a cheat, and to so little purpose.

She picks up a herbiary, opens it, looks at the drawings within. Some feel familiar, though she can't read the words beside them—a strange, toothy script in a language she hasn't been taught, proceeding from the wrong margin.

"May I help you, my lady," murmurs a voice from her side. She turns to look.

Dark hair and eyes, skin brown as branches. *Beautiful*, feels Blodeuwedd suddenly, in the heart of her, where her breath vanishes; *beautiful*, a strike and a searing, a jagged line of light.

She feels all this before she thinks to ask, "Who are you?"

"My name is Adain, my lady, lately of Penllyn." She smiles. "I am a scholar—I arrived today with your lord, to consult the library. I had heard you were . . . indisposed—"

Blodeuwedd nods. "My apologies for not meeting you on arrival. I've been unwell."

She can't stop looking at Adain's face.

"This book," she says brusquely, holding it out. "What does it say?"

Adain accepts it, looks at the open page. "It is a Levantine treatise on the oak; see, here it speaks of the different parts of the tree and their uses."

"What," she says, pointing, "does this part say?"

"Ah—that the oak is more likely to be struck by lightning than any other tree."

Blodeuwedd grabs the book back suddenly, shuts it with a snap. Her forehead throbs; she turns away, closes her eyes. "Forgive me; I have a terrible headache, and should rest."

She sets the book down, and walks away before Adain can say another word.

"Husband," said Blodeuwedd, hair spread over her pillow like a season, "were you not a man until you had a name, a weapon, and a wife?"

"No, my lady," he said, smiling, running his thumb along her cheek, "I was only a boy."

"You gave me a name; if I had a weapon, and a wife, could I also be a man?"

His laughter scythed a bright, hot line along her chest. "No, my lady."

She wet her lips, and smiled. "Why not?"

"Because you were made by magic, my lady, from flowers."

"I do not understand, my husband," she said carefully. "Magic made you a boy, from your mother, and now you are a man. If I won myself a weapon and a wife, why should I not be a man, and conquer lands to reign over, as you do?"

Lleu thought on that. "It is because," he said finally, "you were made for me, belong to me, and I have decreed that you are my wife. And once you are my wife you can be no other thing."

Blodeuwedd spends a full day abed, sleeping fitfully, twisting her long yellow hair into her fists. The dull ache of hunger in her sharpens itself against thoughts of Adain—she hears her voice again, over and over, saying "my lady," so unlike when Lleu says it, the same words but the meaning as different as day from night, as bird from worm.

How could the same words mean so many things? Rain was rain, and sun was sun, and earth was earth. Only wizards could change one thing into another—honour into shame, maiden into mother, a mother's curses into a wife.

Her head hurts so much.

She instructs her attendants to have breakfast brought to her the next morning, and to summon Adain to share it with her.

When Adain arrives, a book in her hand, the noise in her head subsides.

"I apologize," says Blodeuwedd, gesturing for Adain to sit down, "for my rudeness yesterday. Is there anything you lack?"

"Nothing at all, my lady," says Adain quietly, looking at her. "Except to know the cause of your pain, and whether it is in my power to help with it."

Blodeuwedd shrugs. "It is a small matter that is always with me. But tell me of yourself, of your studies. Where does your interest lie?"

Adain holds her gaze a long moment. "In plants and animals, my lady. The study of natural history."

Silence lengthens like a shadow between them.

"How interesting," says Blodeuwedd at last, politely. "I hope you find many books on the subject."

"My lady," says Adain, lowering her voice, and her gaze, "I came especially because I heard of your own history."

Blodeuwedd holds very still.

"The marvel of Gwynedd," says Adain quietly. "A meadow made maiden. The fairest woman the world has ever known."

"And you wanted to see for yourself," says Blodeuwedd, trying to swallow the thorns in her throat, to keep the bitterness from her voice. "Well—I am as you find me. The work of wizards. A singular specimen."

Adain winces. "My lady, it is I who should apologize—"

"It is well, Adain," she says curtly. "I must beg you to excuse me—it goes ill with me again, and I would lie down."

Adain looks briefly miserable as she stands, and the glimpse of it lashes at Blodeuwedd, a mix of sorrow and triumph. To have caused her pain. To have spilled her own into her.

"I brought you this, my lady," says Adain, holding out the book she brought—a slender quarto volume with a bouquet of lilies embroidered into the cover and spine. "I hoped it might interest you. It speaks of the language of flowers."

Blodeuwedd stares at her. "What do you know of the language of flowers?"

"I know," she says, holding her gaze, "that they hunger for depth and height, for sun and rain, for the touch of insects, and that all men see of them are their pretty colours and sweet smells."

Blodeuwedd looks at the book for a long time. When she senses Adain about to withdraw, she says, "Wait."

Adain does.

"Come closer," she says, and Adain obeys. Blodeuwedd reaches for her and draws her closer still, till she sits near enough that they can bend their foreheads together. Blodeuwedd lifts her hair from the spreading bruise at her brow.

"What can you tell me of this?"

Adain hesitates, hovers her fingers above the bruise. Blodeuwedd watches her, then closes her eyes as Adain touches her.

She shivers, and Adain gasps as petals push past Blodeuwedd's skin, unfurling toward her hand.

The relief of it is unspeakable. Blodeuwedd all but goes limp from it.

"It is an anemone, my lady," breathes Adain, tracing its edges.

Blodeuwedd shakes her head, dazed with how light, how clear it feels. "That can't be. I was only made of three flowers."

"Aye, and people are made of flesh and blood and bone, but that isn't what comes out of our mouths in speech. You—" Adain looks at her with such tenderness that Blodeuwedd can't bear it, looks away. "Have you been biting your tongue all this time, my lady?"

Blodeuwedd bites her lip in answer, hardly hearing Adain over the peace of her body, the absence of pain. She fixes her eyes on the book Adain brought. "Tell me, then—what do anemones mean?"

"They signify fading hope and loss. But"—Adain brushes Blodeuwedd's hair away from the flower, smiles—"they are also said to mean anticipation."

"How," whispers Blodeuwedd, looking back to her, "do we know which it is?"

Adain holds her gaze while her fingers work delicately beneath the bloom.

"Context," she says, and plucks it.

There came a day when Lleu was knocked from his horse in war, shot through with many arrows, but he survived, prevailed, and his borders widened.

There came a day when Lleu was gored by a great boar during a hunt, but he survived, slew it, made a brush of its bristles for Blodeuwedd's hair.

There came a day when Blodeuwedd watched Lleu's naked body as he slept and made a knife of her eyes, a tusk of her teeth, and imagined unseaming his belly, imagined ripping into the meat of him and feasting on his heat. She made a noise deep in her throat, and his eyes opened, and she murmured, wanting him to hear—

"Can nothing kill you, Lleu?"

He smiled at her, and when he spoke his words had the ring of enchantment, incantation.

"I cannot be killed day or night, inside or outside, on horseback or on foot. I cannot be killed clothed or naked, nor by any weapon honourably made."

Blodeuwedd's chin trembled before her mouth made a smile of it.

"Then my husband is immortal, and shall never be parted from me."

"Just so, my lady." He laughed, bright as his name. "Unless the Almighty sees fit to dress me in netting and have me straddle a goat's back and a bathtub's edge by the side of a river at dusk, with a thickly thatched curve of roof above the tub, while a man stabs at me with a spear made of a year of Sundays. But if I were meant to die, would Fate have made my killing so difficult to arrange? Rejoice, then, Blodeuwedd, for you'll never be rid of me."

In the weeks that follow, Blodeuwedd and Adain are inseparable: reading in the library, walking along the grounds, sharing meals, sharing beds. Blodeuwedd cannot get enough of her, seeks always to be touching her, murmurs questions over their clasped hands and into the warmth of her neck.

"What does this mean," she asks, leading Adain's fingers to

every ache in her body. Under her touch a deep red rose buds from her wrist, a bluebell from her breastbone, a heap of lilacs from her ankles, a crush of sweet peas from her nape. Adain opens her mouth in answer against each bloom, until Blodeuwedd's cheeks flush from the heat of her breath, the tip of her tongue tracking light along the petals. Blodeuwedd feels every part of her clamouring to be read.

Adain reads her—but tells her, too, of what's outside her body, of all the plants and animals beyond the walls. Blodeuwedd listens keenly to her stories of the silent flight of owls, the cleverness of crows; the healing to be found in yarrow and willow bark, the soothing properties of raspberry leaf and mint. Blodeuwedd listens, but most thirstily for lessons on foxglove and mistletoe, hemlock and yew.

"These are plants that kill," Blodeuwedd says, astonished. "Plants that hide weapons inside them."

"In a sense. Though many poisons can heal if properly diluted and applied," says Adain. "A needle can stab and it can stitch; the same property can harm or heal. It is all a matter of context, of degree. Some poisons even heal each other's effects! Belladonna is dangerous, but it's also an antidote to wolfsbane." She smiles, just a little wan. "And anything is poison if you have too much of it."

The silence that follows her words has a shadow beneath its skin. Blodeuwedd sees it, reaches for it, gently.

"Is this too much, Adain? Am I poisoning you?"

"No," she says, swiftly, "no. Only I know this cannot last beyond your lord's return."

Blodeuwedd stills—then shrugs. "He is more often away than he is here. I am told he is at war, and while he will never die, he may yet be months, perhaps even a year away."

"But while he is here—"

"I will be bored, and hungry, and in pain, as I was before. But I will know you are here, and that will be—something. Better, if not enough."

Adain looks as if she would say something else—but Blodeuwedd's face is smooth, pleasant, any pain folded away behind it like a crocus in rain. When Adain rests a hand on Blodeuwedd's shoulder, a whole hood of aconite stretches into her palm like a cat.

Blodeuwedd took to playing a pillow game with Lleu: she would hold a knife to his neck or stomach, spit her hatred of him, and cut into him while he moaned. The cuts never went deeper than paper, no matter where she dragged the blade. Sometimes they played with rope, sometimes with fire; each time, Lleu trembled and cried out, lay spent and panting and infuriatingly alive.

He loved the games, though, and how she never played the same way twice.

"Shall I tell you," says Adain one day, as they walk together in the orchard, hand in hand, "about the flowers of which you were made?"

Blodeuwedd shrugs. "Those I know—meadowsweet for scent, broom for tidiness, oak for hospitality."

Adain shakes her head. "Those are only parts—"

"They only used parts. The blossoms, they said. There is nothing in me of root, thorn, branch—nothing that digs, cuts, climbs."

Adain looks at her sidelong, then back ahead, frowning.

"That may be, my lady," she says finally. "But blossoms carry seeds, and in that contain the whole of the plant. So I shall tell you all the same."

She stops walking, and Blodeuwedd stops with her; Adain crouches down, indicating Blodeuwedd's feet and legs.

"Meadowsweet is always underfoot, but the more it's bruised, the more scent it gives off; there is defiance in that, I think, like a song that won't be stopped up."

Adain touches Blodeuwedd's legs through the fine cloth that covers them, standing slowly, working her way up. Blodeuwedd closes her eyes, feeling something like a breeze rustling the leaves and stems inside her.

"Broom," Adain continues, gesturing to Blodeuwedd's middle.

"You know about the thorns, and it has a sweet smell too, but it's most notable for thriving in poor soil. It survives where little else could."

She places a palm over Blodeuwedd's heart. "And oak—"

"Is more likely," Blodeuwedd whispers, opening her eyes and covering Adain's hand with hers, "to be struck by lightning than any other tree of the same height."

"Full marks," says Adain, and stands on her toes to kiss her. "You were made of flowers, my love, but those are only pieces of you, the seeds from which you grew. You—you cannot be pressed into a book. You are so much more than the work of wizards."

Blodeuwedd is quiet for a space. Then she asks, "Are you a wizard, Adain?"

Adain blinks, then laughs. "Not at all! Why do you ask?"

"You . . . changed me, as they did. They saw plants, and made a woman—soft, sweet, biddable. You see the same plants, and make a different woman—hard, sharp, strong. How?"

"I like to think I see you as you are," she says, "and they see what they want to see. What flatters their vanity."

"Or am I the one thing when they look at me, the other when you do?" She chews her lip.

"Which do you want to be, my lady?"

"I want," she says, her voice a husk. "I want to eat. I want to change others. I want no one to tell me who or what I am, what I can or cannot be. I want"—she draws closer to Adain, wraps her arms around her, snakes her fingers into Adain's hair and tugs until she gasps—"to take what I please when I'm hungry, to ask no leave. I want a wife, and a weapon."

She releases Adain's hair, steps back. She looks at the ground.

"I want to be a wizard, though I hate them as I have never hated anything else."

"Is it a wizard you want to be," says Adain, looking up at her, "or a wizard's power you want to have?"

She chuckles. "Can I have the one without the other?"

"Certainly. Wizards—their power lies in naming. They shape reality because they tell a good story. Tell a different one—one of your choosing, one of your desire—and teach it to the world until it learns your truth and makes room for it."

Blodeuwedd raises an eyebrow. "That sounds like a pretty story itself."

"You were flowers, and they made you a woman," says Adain firmly. She hesitates for a moment, like an autumn leaf in a stiff wind before resolving to fall. "I too was once other than I am. I had a different name; I threw a mighty spear; I was lord of Penllyn, and did not want to be. And I gave them up—my name, my weapons, my lands—to be a woman among books, a woman among women. To be the blossom on the gorse instead of the thorn."

Blodeuwedd listens, and there is wonder in it, that Adain could ever have been other than she is; that Blodeuwedd, for all her failed hours in the orchard mud, could yet be something else—could be what she desired, instead of what she was before choice was taken from her.

"Teach me," she says at last. "Teach me how."

When Lleu returns from his business abroad, Blodeuwedd receives him as she never has before: there is a spark in her eyes she knows will thrill him, and her smile bares more teeth than she usually shows. She sees him surprised, and pleased.

"My lady," he says, "I've missed you," and leans forward to kiss her on both cheeks.

As he does, she whispers, "I've thought of a new game to play."

His eyes widen, and he grins, and sheds his armour as swiftly as is seemly, then follows where she leads.

"Not to the bedchamber," she says, coy. "I've thought of something much better."

She leads him out past the inner walls, and the outer; assures him there isn't far to go, until they arrive at the river.

There is a cauldron there, half-covered with a thatched roof; next to it is a placid goat, an old fishing net.

"Blodeuwedd," he whispers, "what's this?"

"I want it to feel more real," she says smoothly. "The possibility of your death. Take off your clothes, husband."

He does as she says, tensing with desire and fear. She drapes the fishing net over him.

"Now," she says, "onto the goat."

"You don't have a spear," he observes.

She smiles. "I don't need one." She dips a tin cup into the cauldron, offers it to him. "Drink, my husband. We have thirsty work ahead."

Lleu does as he's told, keeping his balance on goat and tub the while.

As he drinks, she says, "Do you know what today is, husband?"

He hesitates, wiping his mouth. "Sunday, my lady."

"So it is. I've had much more than a year of them, you know, in your house—biting my tongue, speaking in flowers neither of us could read. I could have made you a whole other wife," she chuckles, "from the foxgloves I pulled from my fingers, the aconite I brushed from my hair. But I have learned something of my roots, while you were away."

Lleu frowns—coughs. He shakes his head, makes as if to step down.

"Stay," she says, "exactly where you are."

"Blodeuwedd—"

"Have you ever heard me speak so many words to you?" she wonders. "Have you ever thought to ask what I thought, what I wanted, what I needed, when you took me from my home and planted me in yours?"

"You are my *wife*," he gasps, and stumbles. The goat bleats in sudden panic as he loses his footing, falls backward, half into the river. Blodeuwedd watches him like an owl, but does not move. Lleu opens his mouth to speak further, but his tongue is swollen. His brow is fevered and wet. Blodeuwedd can hear his heart beating in furious rhythms.

"Adain!" she calls. "Adain, come out!"

Adain emerges from the trees, carrying another cup; she hurries to Lleu's side.

"Not yet," says Blodeuwedd, sharp as needles. "Lleu Llaw Gyffes, I am not your wife. Swear it now, and Adain will give you an antidote."

Lleu shakes his head, coughs blood—for a moment. Then he looks at Adain, and looks at Blodeuwedd, and nods. "I swear it," he spits through swollen lips.

"Swear," says Blodeuwedd, "that you will never take another wife, never make your manhood from another's pain."

Lleu stares for a long moment.

"*Swear!*" hisses Adain.

"I—swear—"

"Swear," says Blodeuwedd, "that you will never raise arms against me or mine, nor let your uncles seek to harm us in any way."

"I swear," he says in a voice of milkweed floss, more breath than words, and there is a sorrow in his eyes that makes her almost hate him less.

She nods, and Adain tips the antidote into the red of his mouth.

Blodeuwedd steps forward, squats down next to him as he pants. She dips her sleeve in the river, uses it to wipe the sweat from his brow.

"You gathered flowers and read *woman*. You read *woman* and gleaned docile, pretty, fragrant, weak. But you misread me, Lleu. I have in me the hearts of great ships, the bones of cathedrals. I have in me the sharpness of claws. And you, Lleu, what do you have? You cling like ivy. You smother like mistletoe. But what are you, besides wizard's work?"

She stands again, looks down at him.

"I will never again be what I was before you. But I will be *more*. And you—you will be a rogue, a rascal. You will be anything but a man."

Lleu cries out, pours his pain onto the air as Blodeuwedd never could. As she and Adain watch, Lleu's shape shrinks, shifts, blurs at the edges, as the magic called *man* leaves him, as he fights to hold on to it. A light flares from him, then dims. All that's left tangled in the net is a hawk, sour of body, sound of wing; no sooner do they lift the net's coils than the bird springs into the air, crying.

Blodeuwedd watches him go, speechless. She stares at Adain.

"I . . . did not know that would happen," she says. "Are all men hawks, without wives?"

"There was magic in his making, and magic in his unmaking,"

says Adain, looking up at the sky. "His uncles will know soon enough what happened, but his vows will bind them no matter his shape."

Then Adain draws her close, kisses her.

"You did it," she says. "You're free."

Blodeuwedd nods, silent, gazing into the darkness after Lleu's wings.

"Free," Adain insists, "from everything—from retaliation, from his uncles. You could rule his house if you wanted; you could come back with me to the abbey—we could keep studying together, make a life." Adain takes her hand. "You have everything you wanted—a name, a weapon—"

"Adain." Blodeuwedd kisses her. "I think we can do better than that."

The moon rises fat and bright over the river; Blodeuwedd looks at its reflection on the water rippling the coin of it into white and silver lines.

"I want to meet Arianrhod," she says at last. "My former mother-in-law. I want to know what she's like. Will you come with me? Before you answer," she says, cutting off the passion in Adain's eyes, "I cannot say whether I will stay as I am, now that you've taught me to read between my lineaments. I may hunger again. I may change."

"I wouldn't have you any other way," says Adain firmly. "And so long as you'll have me, I will stay with you to the earth's end."

Adain kisses her hand, then turns from the water, and begins calling gently for the goat.

Blodeuwedd takes her time before following; she stretches her hand out in the moonlight, turns her wrist to the sky. She feels no blooming pressure there, or anywhere. Nothing hurts.

For the first time, the blue branches of her veins look like roots.

POCKETS

The first strange thing Nadia pulled from her pocket was a piece of fudge. It was a perfectly ordinary piece of fudge. It was only that Nadia hated fudge, and couldn't imagine how she'd come to be carrying it around. She remembered this in particular because it was a bright, cool autumn day and she'd dug into her jacket pocket instinctively, looking for change to leave in a busker's open violin case, and had come upon the piece of fudge instead. After staring at it awkwardly for a moment, she dropped it into the violin case and hurried away before she could see whether the busker was scowling at her or not.

She didn't think about the fudge again until a few days later, when, fumbling for her wallet at the grocery store, her hand closed on an unfamiliar tube of lipstick. It was unfamiliar in several respects: first, Nadia didn't keep lipstick in her jacket pocket; second, on inspection it was a bright, light red that Nadia would never have chosen for herself, favouring plums and burgundies; and third—it just didn't *feel* like hers. Nadia knew her own things. She could pick out her nondescript, utterly generic black cloth suitcase from among the dozens piling up in airport luggage carousels purely by that feel of the familiar, that tug of touch, of knowing its contours, its frayed threads and worn wheels.

She'd never been anywhere with this lipstick. It was half-used, too; Nadia found herself imagining a complexion materializing around the mouth that had worn this colour—carnelian, she thought, in the absence of a brand name. She found herself leaning towards her reflection in a furniture store window, thinking to try it—but stopped, frowning, and capped the tube. She took it home, placed it in her bathroom, and found herself looking at it every morning while she brushed her teeth, wondering.

The third strange thing Nadia pulled from her pocket was an

antique map of Syria. It was rolled up tightly, and her cold fingers strained clumsily against its curling edges. By now she was certain someone was playing a trick on her, slipping things into her pockets when she wasn't paying attention. She decided she was willing to play along for a while. She took the map home, rolled up and secured with a bit of ribbon, and placed it on her desk. After a moment, she went into the bathroom, retrieved the lipstick, and put it down next to the map.

The fourth thing was a coin, old and worn; whatever face or figure had been stamped on it was long faded. Nadia found it in the pocket of her jeans while reaching for her door key. She put it next to the map, arranging and re-arranging the collection, sometimes standing the map up, sometimes laying it down with the lipstick in front of it, sometimes poking both lipstick and coin into the hollow cylinder it made.

She wondered if she ought to have kept the fudge.

Over the next few days Nadia looked for clues as to who was playing this game with her. She tried to drop casual hints around friends, who looked confused; when she tried outright asking if they were putting things in her pockets, they looked amused, or offended. She stopped asking.

The objects, she felt, were becoming more esoteric. She pulled out what looked like a pin made of bone from the pocket of a cardigan; a stiff-bristle paintbrush from a flimsy decorative trouser pocket that should certainly have been too small for it; a single chopstick from an inside jacket pocket; an old-looking bath plug and chain from the pocket of her favourite dress (favourite, heretofore, because it had pockets). She arranged them all on her desk, making more and more space for them, feeling more and more helpless as the pile grew.

One evening, as she undressed, she found herself pulling a gun from her trousers—a flintlock pistol, its lobed stock of dark wood ornamented with chased brass mounts.

The gun smelled strongly of having just been fired.

She decided to stop wearing pockets.

Nadia walked along the river with her friend, only half listening to Tessa while breathing on her thinly gloved hands, rubbing them together in the cold air. She could see the moisture from her breath crystallizing on the gloves' loose fibres.

When Tessa asked "Why don't you just put your hands in your pockets?" she winced.

"I can't," she muttered.

Tessa blinked. "What? Why not?"

"I—um. I sewed them shut."

"What!"

Nadia shrugged. "They were . . . tearing. It's not usually a problem, I have tons of gloves, I just thought it'd be warmer today."

"They were tearing on the inside so you sewed them *shut*?"

"Can we not talk about this?" said Nadia, angrily. "It's winter, my hands are cold, whatever."

Tessa looked like she'd been slapped, and slowed her pace a bit. Nadia suddenly felt a stab of guilt, one that sank deep into her belly as she watched Tessa tug off her mittens—big woolly things Nadia had knitted her a year ago—and hold them out to her quietly.

Nadia's eyes glistened. "I'm sorry. I just—I'm sorry," she said, taking the mittens and slipping them on. "Thank you."

"You've been so distracted lately," said Tessa, quietly. "Just let me know if you want to talk about it, OK?"

Nadia said nothing for a long moment.

"If I tell you," she said, looking her friend in the eye, "you have to promise to believe me."

Tessa was a biologist in training. Nadia braced herself for the skepticism, the scrutiny, the razor of Tessa's inquiring mind slicing through the half-formed thoughts Nadia had about what was happening.

But Tessa didn't even hesitate. "I promise," she said.

Nadia breathed deeply and exhaled slowly. Then, handing Tessa back her mittens, she pressed one hand against the side of her coat, and with the other began to break the stitches keeping the pocket shut.

Then she reached into her pocket and pulled out a trombone.

They spent the afternoon organizing tests in the Biology Department's student labs: it warmed Nadia's heart to see Tessa brimming with excitement, dressing her in one of Tessa's university-issued lab coats while burbling about thermodynamics and conservation of mass.

"So," she beamed, "if we weigh you with the lab coat pockets empty, and then you pull something out of your pocket and your weight equals Nadia plus Object, then in order not to violate the law, we have to suppose the object was somehow taken from elsewhere."

"Oh." Nadia frowned. She didn't like the thought that she was *taking* things from elsewhere—she didn't want them, after all. She'd come to think of the objects as intrusions in her life, not something she'd removed from someone or someplace else.

"If, on the other hand," Tessa continued, "you pull something out of your pocket and your weight doesn't change, then the object must've somehow been deducted from your mass."

"Wait, what?" Nadia stared. "You mean, like—I'd be *turning into* trombones and fudge and maps? That they're made out of me?"

"No, no," said Tessa, laughing, "don't be silly, that'd be magic."

"But then—"

"Just get on the scale, hon."

Nadia did so, shuddering at the thought of shedding pieces of herself one half-used tube of lipstick at a time.

"Are you still cold?" asked Tessa, sympathetically.

"No, I'm fine. Let's do this."

"Right, 70.534 kg—" Tessa made a note. "Now—pull something out."

Nadia took a deep breath, closed her eyes, reached into the lab coat's pocket, and pulled out—

"OH, er, that's mine," said Tessa hastily, plucking the tampon out of Nadia's hand. "Balls, I'm always leaving stuff in there. Hand me the coat back, I'll take care of it."

Nadia waited while Tessa retrieved two pens, another tampon, and a pair of safety specs from the pockets before handing the coat back. She put it back on, waited for Tessa to note her weight again, then—slowly, carefully—reached into the lab coat.

She felt about with her fingers until they brushed against something round and bumpy. Biting her lip, she pulled out an orange studded with cloves, dry and fragrant.

"A pomander!" said Tess, delighted. "This is amazing. OK, let's look at the scale—"

Nadia held her breath. She wondered if the weight of the soul could be reckoned in fruit and spice.

"—You, my dear, have put on the weight of one pomander." Tessa grinned. "I think we can safely deduce that this is a spatio-temporal issue and not a weird skin condition."

Together they determined that Nadia could only pull things out of pockets she herself was wearing; that a coat draped over one shoulder apparently didn't count as "wearing" after several separate tries; that the objects she produced added to her mass; that they did not vanish if put back in the pockets; and that after a pomander, an ocarina, an empty plastic bag, a dry peach pit, a drop spindle, a broken hockey stick, an empty fountain pen, a small gnome, and a pack of wooden playing cards, they were no closer to learning where the objects were coming from, why they had started appearing in Nadia's pockets, or, most crucially, how to make them stop.

"Tessa," she said, finally, "can we—stop trying to figure out how this is happening and try to figure out why it's happening?"

"Huh?" Tessa blinked. "But we are doing that. I mean, the one will lead to the other eventually—but it's like figuring out the weather. Some days it rains, or snows, or is sunny, right?"

"Sure."

"And if we didn't know about seasons—or climate change—or hot and cold fronts—the weather would seem pretty random, right?"

"Right."

"So, think of this as a weather system of *stuff*. We're trying to figure out why they're coming out of your pockets; but until we find out how that's happening, what the variables are, we can't do much more than guesswork."

"Tessa—" Nadia felt helpless. "That makes perfect sense, but—look, *stuff is coming out of my pockets*. I get that this has all kinds of really neat implications for, I don't know, science, but—I just—I want to stop measuring things and think about it differently? Like, just take the weird thing as read? And go on from there?"

Tessa frowned. "How do you mean?"

"Well—" Nadia gestured to the accumulated objects, which, rather than being in a heap as she'd have put them, were neatly labelled and organized by size for further examination. "—I keep thinking—what if it's a message? What if—however the stuff's ending up in my pockets—what if it's all part of a pattern and I'm just not seeing it? Or—what if it's *me*? What if I woke up with this *power* one day and I'm supposed to be using it for good, to help people, but I can't because I've not figured it out? I just—" The frustration made her throat ache. "I found a *gun* in my pocket, Tessa! That has to mean something, doesn't it?"

Tessa grew quiet. "Okay. I'm sorry—it must be weird to just have me treating you as a problem to be solved. Tell me what you'd like to do and I'll listen."

Nadia thought for a moment. Then she closed her eyes again and pulled out a rectangular cardboard box the length of her forearm. There was a label on the front: "Full Scale, S 6032, Au Clair de la Lune, Op. 30, Variations et final, *Lambert*, ACCENTUATED." Frowning, she lifted the lid.

"It's a piano roll," said Tessa, standing on tiptoe to see into the box. "I've seen Warda stacking them in the Music Department."

". . . Could we . . ." She looked around the lab, not very hopeful of finding a player piano. "Could we go there? Maybe see if we can play this?"

Tessa chewed her lip, but nodded. "Sure."

⁓

Warda had been the university's college support librarian for music for twenty-six years. She spoke English, Arabic, German, French, Swedish, and Russian. She played the piano and three kinds of flute. She had lived in four countries and fled two before settling.

Tessa knew her from flute lessons; Nadia knew her from the occasional question or conversation about music history. Neither could imagine the library without her in it.

Warda looked at the piano roll curiously. "We can certainly play it—it's in good condition. But may I ask why? It's a common tune."

Nadia and Tessa exchanged a look.

"It's . . . an experiment," said Tessa, slowly. Nadia looked at Warda, thoughtfully.

"I . . . found it in a pocket," she said, quietly, and saw something in Warda's expression of mild curiosity shift and tense. "I don't know where it came from."

"I see," said Warda. "May I?"

Nadia held out the roll to her. Warda took it with one hand, and with the other, held open the tiny knitted pocket of her cardigan.

They watched as all twelve inches of the piano roll vanished into the pocket without making so much as a bulge in the fabric.

Warda poured tea for them in her office while Tessa asked question after question.

"When did this start?"

"Oh, a year or so ago, give or take."

"And did you ever lose any of these things?" Tessa showed her a list of things that had come out of Nadia's pockets, but Warda smiled and shook her head.

"No. I see what you're asking, but I don't think it works that way."

"Why not?" asked Nadia.

"I suppose it just doesn't make sense to me that in all the world ours would be the only two pockets connected to each other. Have you read Stoppard's *Arcadia*? 'We shed as we pick up, like travellers who must carry everything in their arms, and what we let fall will be picked up by those behind.'"

"Thermodynamics," murmured Tessa.

"If you like," said Warda, stirring sugar into her tea. "I think of it as leaks—leaks in the universe, and things that plug up those leaks. If one thing vanishes, another has to appear."

"But you don't *know* that," said Nadia, uncertainly.

"No. I just know that I carry my keys and wallet in a purse and thank goodness for the paucity of pockets in women's clothing." She smiled, and Tessa chuckled, but Nadia said nothing.

Warda offered her a mug of tea, gently. "Shall I tell you more of how I think of it?"

Nadia nodded, accepting the mug, spreading her fingers around it and through its ear to absorb as much of its heat as she could.

"I had always wanted to write," said Warda, "when I was a child—words, music. But it was not convenient. When this started happening, I began to write: small things, notes, letters. I wrote 'hello' in different languages; I wrote my email address; I wrote little rhymes. I would roll them up and put them in my pocket and hope that someone would receive them, read them, and want to find me." She chuckled into her tea. "It was a very romantic thought.

"But then I thought, no, it was not about me, ultimately—or it was, but not as I'd imagined. I thought, if there is a leak in my pocket, perhaps someone else's pocket is the opposite. And I thought, perhaps when I write, when I create something out of the nothing—the everything, really—that is because somewhere else, someone else has a need. A leak. A hole in the pocket of their soul. And while I cannot be sure, perhaps my words are what will fill them up. So I have written longer things—letters, stories, songs—whatever I feel moved to write, even if it is poor, shabby stuff. I put my writing in my pockets, and I hope for the best."

"But you never know," said Nadia, again, with an urgency. "There's no way to *know*. What if I'm stealing things from other places without meaning to? What if I'm supposed to use these things somehow, for something important? How"—she exhaled, loudly, frustrated—"how can I know what it *means*?"

"Well," said Warda, sipping her tea, "it has been a year and I have learned this very interesting thing: that I was right about someone else having the equal and opposite sort of pocket. Thanks to you, I know this." Warda smiled, put her hand on Nadia's arm. "And we can only do our best with what we know."

Tessa helped Nadia carry all the things that had come out of her pockets to Warda. They divided them up into things they wanted to keep and things they wanted to pass along. Tessa claimed the pomander; Nadia, after a moment's thought, kept the lipstick;

Warda, biting her lip, took the map of Syria. After that—beginning with the gun, which Nadia still couldn't quite bring herself to look at—they took turns slipping each item into the tiny, decorative, insufficient pocket of Warda's cardigan, and watched as each was swallowed in turn by its fine green knit.

Tessa hugged Nadia as they parted outside the library. Looking at her carefully, she said, "Do you want to borrow my mittens?"

"No thanks," said Nadia, smiling a little. "I think I'll be okay." And as if to prove her point, she slid her hands into the pockets of her coat.

After Tessa was gone, Nadia took a deep breath, closed her eyes, and closed her hand around something. It crinkled in her hand; she pulled out a piece of lined paper with writing on it in blue ink. Smoothing it down as best she could with her thinly gloved hands, she began to read.

She read:

I don't know you, but I wish I did; I wish I could tell you how much I love you, love your eyes for reading this, love your hands for holding my words. I wish I could tell you in a way you would understand that so long as you read this the world is not so terrible a place; that so long as we speak to each other, so long as there is love in the movement of a pen over paper and love in the movement of eyes over words we will be all right, we will know each other, we will learn each other like songs.

Know nothing else of me but that I love you, that I love you as one can only love the unknown conjured by address; that as I speak to you I am inventing you, and that as you read me you are inventing me, and that this is keenly, unspeakably beautiful. Know that whatever else you may be, you are beloved, completely, unconditionally, by me in this space, in this moment, and that this space and this moment will endure ever and always for as long as you read me.

I wrote this for you, for only you, for you alone out of the millions. I love you. Thank you.

ACKNOWLEDGMENTS

I'm writing this accompanied by the sound of rain in autumn, thinking about how many seasons turned in how many places as these stories found their way into the world in various forms before settling into your hands like water and fallen leaves. There are so many people to thank.

First and foremost, my parents, Leila and Oussama, to whom this collection is dedicated. It's no small thing to be encouraged toward the arts from a tender age, and the fact that they considered the act of writing a serious and worthwhile pursuit shaped not only my life's trajectory but my capacity to value my own work. Through them, I want also to thank Jiddo Ajaj and Teta Syria—the grandparents who found their way into so much of this writing. My grandfather was a poet, among many other things; my grandmother was a whole country. I love them all and am so grateful to them. I walk this world by their light.

I want to thank my husband, Stu West, for his constant warmth and support. So many of these stories predate our acquaintance, and every one since has benefited from his scrutiny. Absolutely no one nags me to write as consistently and relentlessly as he does. Shukran habibi.

Deep, heartfelt thanks to my agent, DongWon Song, who signed me nearly a decade ago because of my short fiction; to Devi Pillai, who knows what she did; to my wonderful editors Ali Fisher and Dianna Vega, for their insights, enthusiasm, and flexibility with deadlines, as well as their willingness to add extra hoops to the production process by including Arabic text in these pages. Speaking of which: extra thanks are due to my father for translating "Song for an Ancient City" and "Qahr" into Arabic, in consultation with our dear friend Ahmad Asfahani. My father translated these on his own as gifts to me some years ago, but collaborated with Ammo Ahmad to refresh and develop them further for this collection, and if you don't read Arabic, you'll just have to trust me that they really sing.

I am grateful to and in awe of Jocelyn Bright, Saraciea Fennell, and Khadija Lokhandwala's work in publicity, and of Michael Dudding, Samantha Friedlander, and Eileen Lawrence's work in marketing; by their powers combined, I get to connect with booksellers and readers in meaningful ways, whether at events, on the internet, or through the simple fact of you holding this book in your hands—which is as lovely an object as it is because of Esther Kim, Heather Saunders, and Lauren Hougen, who respectively designed the jacket, designed the interior, and managed production. I truly feel extraordinarily lucky that my work gets to benefit from theirs.

Naming the host of friends who've inspired, improved, and nourished my work over decades is like numbering the stars in the sky, but here are some of the brightest constellations I associate with this collection: Jessica Wick, my first serious reader outside of family (and long since adopted into it), who spurred me to write and read short fiction alongside her; Terri Windling, whose presence in the world holds open a door to enchantment; Charles de Lint, Pat Caven, and Margo MacDonald, whose early encouragements were foundational to a bright-eyed, book-loving teenager; C. S. E. Cooney, Caitlyn Paxson, Nicole Kornher-Stace, and Patty Templeton, my beautiful Banjo Apocalypse Crinoline Troubadours, for joyful, generative collaboration; Karen Meisner and Pär Winzell, whose friendship and hospitality have enriched my writing and my life; Neil Williamson, Tessa Kum, Elaine Gallagher, and everyone in the Glasgow Science Fiction Writing Circle circa 2014 who swung by the staircase in Eastercon to cheer me on in writing my first real science fiction story. Max Gladstone, dear friend and partner in so many crimes, helped fix the title story by reminding me to think more deeply about time.

There are editors, too, without whom many of these stories wouldn't exist: Christie Yant and Julia Rios, who wouldn't let me not write them stories because I was scared; Dominik Parisien, who improves everything he looks upon and is so generous with his gaze, and whose editorial collaborations with Navah Wolfe drew out two stories in this collection; Jonathan Strahan, whose enthusiasm and encouragement have been so moving to me. I truly can't recall at this moment if I've ever turned a story in by the first deadline given to me, so the fact that any of my work is published at all is testament to the ingenuity and patience of people willing to put up with me and my (long-possessed but only recently diagnosed) ADHD. I want also to thank Mike Allen and R. B. Lemberg, editors of poetry magazines *Mythic Delirium* and *Stone Telling*, who made a home for so much good and beautiful poetry over the years, and generously welcomed my own.

Weather turns as seasons do; I'm finishing this accompanied by the warmth of sun in autumn, listening to squirrels nibble through the hulls of black walnuts while scolding neighbourhood cats.

There are people whom I would thank if our friendship had survived their inability to see me as a whole person. I mention this now to say: no friendship should survive that. As I write we are two years into witnessing Israel committing genocide against the Palestinian people, through manufactured famine and US-funded bombs. Any person or publication refusing, at the barest possible minimum, to acknowledge and condemn this is not one with whom I can feel any bond of fellowship or solidarity. I can only wish them the restoration of their souls and hope to welcome them, in time, to the work of liberation and the justice of witches.

To everyone already there with me: thank you, from the deepest parts of my heart.

COPYRIGHT ACKNOWLEDGMENTS

"Seasons of Glass and Iron." *The Starlit Wood: New Fairy Tales*, New York: Saga Press, 2016.

"The Green Book." *Apex Magazine*, November 2010.

"Madeleine." *Lightspeed*, June 2015.

"The Lonely Sea in the Sky." *Lightspeed*, June 2014.

"Song for an Ancient City." *Mythic Delirium*, Winter 2008.

"And Their Lips Rang with the Sun." *Strange Horizons*, October 2009.

"A Tale of Ash in Seven Birds." *The Djinn Falls in Love & Other Stories*, Oxford: Solaris Books, 2017.

"Qahr." *AmalElMohtar.com*, December 2023.

"The Truth About Owls." *Kaleidoscope: Diverse YA, Science Fiction and Fantasy Stories*, Yokine, WA: Twelfth Planet Press, 2014.

"Wing." *Strange Horizons*, December 2012.

"A Hollow Play." *Glitter & Mayhem*, Lexington, KY: Apex Book Company, 2013.

"Thunderstorm in Glasgow, July 25, 2013." *Fireside*, January 2018.

"Anabasis." *Tor.com*, March 2017.

"To Follow the Waves." *Steam-Powered: Lesbian Steampunk Stories*, Rio Rancho, NM: Torquere Press, 2011.

"Pieces." *Stone Telling*, 2011.

"John Hollowback and the Witch." *The Book of Witches*, New York: Harper Voyager, 2023.

"Florilegia; Or, Some Lies About Flowers." *The Mythic Dream*, New York: Saga Press, 2019.

"Pockets." *Uncanny Magazine*, January 2015.

ABOUT THE AUTHOR

Ainslie Coghill

Amal El-Mohtar is a Hugo Award–winning author of science fiction, fantasy, poetry, and criticism, and the coauthor of the *New York Times* bestseller *This Is How You Lose the Time War*, written with Max Gladstone, which has been translated into more than ten languages. Her reviews and articles have appeared in *The New York Times* and on NPR Books. She lives in Ottawa, Canada.